LATE FAME

ARTHUR SCHNITZLER

LATE FAME

Translated from the German
by Alexander Starritt

PUSHKIN PRESS

LONDON

Pushkin Press
71–75 Shelton Street
London WC2H 9JQ

Original text © Paul Zsolnay Verlag Wien 2014
By permission of the Syndics of Cambridge University Library

English translation © Alexander Starritt 2015

Late Fame was first published in the original
German as *Später Ruhm* in 2014

First published by Pushkin Press in 2015

ISBN 978 1 782271 32 1

0 0 1

Frontispiece: *Arthur Schnitzler*, by Ferdinand Schmutzer

Set in Monotype Baskerville by Tetragon, London
Proudly printed and bound in Great Britain by TJ International,
Padstow, Cornwall, on Munken Premium White 90gsm

www.pushkinpress.com

LATE FAME

H ERR EDUARD SAXBERGER came home from his walk and climbed slowly up the stairs to his apartment. It had been a lovely winter's day and as soon as office hours ended, the old gentleman had set off as he often did to stroll around in the fresh air, going far beyond the suburbs to the very last of the houses. He was a little tired and looking forward to his warm and friendly room.

The housekeeper met him with the news that a young man she'd never seen before had been waiting for half an hour. Curious, the old gentleman, who almost never had visitors, went into the sitting room. As he entered, the young man stood up from an armchair and bowed to him.

Saxberger reciprocated the bow and said, "I'm told you've already been waiting for some time—how can I help you?"

The young man remained standing and replied, "Esteemed Herr Saxberger, please allow me to introduce myself. My name is Wolfgang Meier, author."

"Pleased, very pleased to meet you, won't you take a seat?"

"Herr Saxberger," the young man began after he had sat down, "First of all, I must apologize for being so presumptuous as to enter your home unknown and uninvited. But I'd searched in vain for a different way of making your distinguished acquaintance."

"You flatter me."

"And for quite some time, Herr Saxberger, making your acquaintance has been one of my, or rather our, most fervent wishes—because what I'm saying here is not only in my own name."

Herr Meier accompanied these words with a friendly smile. Saxberger sized him up. He was pale, with simple blond hair, and very respectably dressed. While he spoke, he played with a pince-nez that hung on a black cord round his neck. "I'm intrigued," said Herr Saxberger, "by why this fervent wish... since when this fervent wish..." he interrupted himself in embarrassment.

"For some time," answered Meier, "and, to be more precise, I would say: since the day when I, or rather we"— here he again gave a friendly smile—"had the privilege of encountering your *Wanderings*."

"What?" Herr Saxberger cried out in amazement.

"You've read my *Wanderings*? People still read my *Wanderings*?" He shook his head.

"*People* might not read them any more," replied the young man. "But *we* read them, we admire them and, I think, in time, *people*, too, will again come to read and admire them." As Herr Meier spoke in this way, his cheeks flushed a little and his voice became more animated than before.

"You astonish me, Herr… Meier," said Saxberger, "and I would very much like to know who you are, I mean those in whose name you're speaking. I had no idea that anyone today still knew my *Wanderings*." The old gentleman stared into space—"Even I haven't thought of them, it's been so long since I thought of them. For years, I've been so far from any of these things, so far."

Herr Wolfgang Meier smiled delicately. "It hasn't escaped my, or, I should say, *our*, attention, dear sir, that you haven't committed anything to print for a long time, something that surprised and saddened us. And it was, after all, just chance that led us—though here I can probably say *me*—to discover your exquisite book, so to speak, anew."

Saxberger found the words he heard singularly moving. Was this young man really speaking about him? Was it truly possible that this young man, a complete stranger, knew about him and his forgotten work? "How did you come across the book?" he asked.

"It was very straightforward," replied Wolfgang Meier. "I was having a look around a second-hand bookshop and among the books I picked up was your slim volume. As soon as I read the first poems, they had an indescribably powerful effect on me. I took the book home and read it straight through, which as you know hardly ever happens with a collection of poems. When I looked at the title page again and saw the year 1853, I said to myself: you could have known this man—that same evening, I took the book with me to our little circle…"

"What circle is that?"

"It's a group of young writers who stay apart from those following the beaten track. If I said their names, it wouldn't tell you much. These names are not yet known. We are simply artists, no more than that, and our time will come." Herr Meier said these words in a tone that was calm but categorical.

The old gentleman listened attentively, nodding. It was so peculiar. Artists, artists—how that word sounded! All at once there rose up in him muddled images of distant days and forgotten people. Names occurred to him, and what had become of them—and then he saw himself as you see yourself in a dream, as a young man, saw himself youthful, laughing, talking, as one of the best and proudest in a circle of young people who stayed apart from those following the beaten track and did not want to be anything but artists—and he said aloud, as if the young man opposite him had had these rapid thoughts along with him, "That is long ago, that is so long ago!"

Wolfgang Meier observed the old gentleman in silence; only the eyes in that wrinkled, beardless face seemed to have remained young, and these now looked past the small lamp standing on the table and out through the window into the dark-blue night.

"1853"—said Meier after a short pause, "that certainly is a long time ago," and then he continued more spiritedly, "You wouldn't believe, dear sir, how pleased we were when we learnt that the poet of the *Wanderings* was living in our city; it felt as if we had a debt to repay to you." With these words Meier rose and, bowing slightly, said in a solemn voice: "The youth of Vienna ask that you be so good as to accept, through me, their most deeply respectful greetings and their thanks."

Saxberger wanted to get up, but the young man pressed him amiably back into his chair. His voice charged with emotion, Saxberger answered, "Thank you, I don't know, no, I really don't know…"—he stopped speaking, and the young man quietly looked him in the eye with an encouraging smile until he carried on: "It's so long ago—I… I… I don't know anything about it any more, no one thought much of it back then. I haven't written anything for so long. You see, no one takes any notice and then, by and by, I lost my appetite for it, you understand, along with my youth. And also there were worries, the daily work, it all ended so much of its own accord that I didn't even notice…"

The young man listened… he shook his head, commiserating, serious.

"And I did write other things, too, oh yes, not just verse. I once even wrote a play."

"What?" exclaimed Meier, "a play! But, please, where is it? Please!"

"I don't know, I really don't know. My God, I sent it round the theatres at the time—three years it must have done the rounds, or four. Then, well, I let it go. That's more than thirty years ago…"

After saying nothing for a moment, Meier stood up and, while resting one hand on the back of the chair, burst out: "It's the same old story. At the start, we're satisfied to have just our own pleasure in our work and the interest of the few who understand us. But when you see those coming up around you, winning a name and even fame for themselves—then you would rather be heard and honoured as well. And then come the disappointments! The envy of the talentless, the frivolity and malice of reviewers, and then the horrid indifference of the public. And you get tired, tired, tired. You still have a lot you could say, but nobody wants to hear it, and eventually you yourself forget that you were once one of those who wanted great things, who have perhaps even already achieved them."

Saxberger accompanied the young man's words with a slow nod of agreement. Yes, that was exactly how it had been. He had just needed this young man to come and remind him.

"But," said Meier, "I don't want to take up any more of your valuable time."

"Oh, my time isn't valuable," responded Saxberger with a melancholy smile… "When my office hours are over, I don't have anything else to do."

"So you have an office job?" Meier asked with polite interest. "I imagine you can't find that particularly satisfying?"

"Oh, goodness me, my dear man, you get used to it, and what would I do all day if I didn't have a profession?"

"So you're… content?"

"I actually can't complain. I can't actually imagine my life as any different—I ask you, when you've been in a post for almost thirty-five years. Yes, yes," he affirmed as Meier shook his head incredulously, "I've long been able to celebrate my office jubilees!"

"But at the beginning, when you still… wrote, this monotonous employment must have been extremely painful for you."

"Well, everyone has to have some occupation. It's not so bad. Though the opportunities for promotion could be better, that has to be said. But things are good for me, I really can't complain." The old gentleman nodded good-naturedly. "When I started," he continued, "yes, you're quite right, it wasn't how it is now. You've reminded me. It's quite true that there was a time—" he smiled—"when I didn't like to go to the office."

"Is that so?" cried the young man, pleasantly moved.

"When I used to be a 'poet', you're right, you're right, I would sometimes even be absent without any kind of excuse."

"Oh, I understand that so well!" exclaimed Wolfgang Meier. "The *Wanderings* couldn't have been written while you sat in your office day after day. You can hear in those proud verses that they were made by someone who had cast off the shackles of the everyday."

"A lovely time, a lovely time," said the old gentleman, and sank back into his thoughts.

"What message can I give my friends?" Meier asked ebulliently.

"Please thank them, thank them very warmly. Please say that I was very pleased, and that it was so unexpected. It's touched me. Tell them I honestly didn't believe there was anyone in the world who still knew my name—apart, of course, from my colleagues in the office. And send them all my regards, and perhaps they will have more luck than I did."

"Herr Saxberger, perhaps I could be so bold as to ask whether you might, sometime when it's convenient, devote one of your spare afternoons to us?"

"It would be a pleasure," replied Saxberger, "to meet your friends and thank them in person."

"Then I'll try my luck again one evening soon."

Meier said goodbye to the old gentleman, who accompanied him to the door. "My most heartfelt thanks again for the kind reception," said the young man when he was already standing in the stairwell.

"Send my regards to them, all your friends, send my best regards," Saxberger called after him.

Then he went back into his room. He shook his head, laughing. It seemed strange to him when he thought that, in an hour, he would be sitting at his usual place in the Pickled Pear, as though nothing had happened.

The next day, Herr Saxberger received through the post a little volume on whose title page were the words: *Poems* by Wolfgang Meier. On the first inside page he had written in ink: "To the poet of the *Wanderings*, with heartfelt gratitude, the author". That's an elegant gesture, thought the old gentleman, and laid the little book on his desk, resolving to read it that evening. Poems! Who would have predicted it? For years he had read only the newspaper and, before going to sleep, perhaps some "popular" novel.

When he came home after lunch that day and stretched out on the divan, he began to immerse himself in Wolfgang Meier's poetry. Ah! This was by no means as easy as a popular novel. That much was obvious to him after only the first few verses. Saxberger read with great conscientiousness; he read all the more carefully and concentratedly the harder it became for him to form any clear opinion of the poems. He became very anxious. One thing seemed beyond question: they were pretty verses—but when he asked himself what more he might say about them, he found himself at a loss. He came to a poem that tried to portray a landscape. (And here he felt he was seeing more deeply into the work.) It had a stronger effect on him than the earlier ones, which had sung the praises of beautiful girls. Something in him resonated with it. He loved nature. And the older he had become, the greater his love for it had grown. He had discovered new ties to it by which he had not previously been connected. Oh, it was true—love, youth—that was all in the past. And so there was little that those verses could mean to him. What did the high spirits and the triumphs of youth have to do with him these days? How many years had it been since he'd been interested in those things, since he'd even noticed anything of them? He stood alone in the world. Had never been married, never had children—all connection to youth had been lost as he slowly grew older. All his social intercourse was with friends—who grew old as he did.

And as he leafed further and there were more verses telling him about beautiful blue eyes and tender evenings, a bitter feeling crept over him. He lowered the book and stared into the distance.

He wondered what he was supposed to say to Herr Wolfgang Meier on his next visit. He couldn't tell him that he hadn't—well, hadn't what?—hadn't understood it? Not understood it!

Saxberger was almost frightened. He, the poet of the *Wanderings*, didn't understand the verses of Herr Meier! He paced up and down the room a few times. He lit the lamp. And then, tentatively and smiling a little to himself, he opened the bookcase and bent down in front of it. On the lowest shelf, under old magazines and brochures, there must still be a copy, or even two or three, of the *Wanderings*.

Yes, there they were. More than three. He still had six copies. But it was remarkable. He had, naturally, seen these slight volumes many times in years past. He must also have taken them in his hand and—never noticed them. His memory held a false picture of how they looked. He still imagined the *Wanderings* as when they, just published, had been set out in the display windows of a few book-shops. A dark-green, slender volume on whose cover the title was printed in pale letters that were tall but narrow. But the book he held in his hand was blue and the letters were small. And he realized something else: he had seen the books countless times and yes, he recognized them when he saw them… but he simply no longer had the feeling that said: these are the *Wanderings*, which I myself, which I wrote!

He sat at his desk, adjusted the lamp and opened one of the copies. How long it had been since he last looked inside!

The edges were yellowed, the type seemed old-fashioned. He began to read. The first verses were unfamiliar. But as he read only a little further on, his memory stirred to life. It was as if some familiar music were coming closer and closer. And soon not so much as a word was unknown to him. He began to declaim under his breath and nodded along the way you do when listening to something you already know.

So these—these were the *Wanderings* for which the youth of Vienna had yesterday sent him their thanks. Had he deserved them? He would not have been able to say. The whole sorry life that he had led now passed through his mind. Never had he felt so deeply that he was an old man, that not only the hopes, but also the disappointments lay far behind him. A dull hurt rose up in him. He put the book aside, he could not read on. He had the feeling that he had long since forgotten about himself.

On the two following afternoons, Saxberger poked through the lower shelves of his bookcase. There he found old periodicals in which poems of his had once appeared, yellowed manuscripts in his own hand and also newspapers in which were printed the verses of youthful peers whose names came back to him only piecemeal. None of them had really made anything of it, none had become well known. And as for him? He had for many years been no more than Saxberger the civil servant, and had thought no more of being anything else. Sometimes he had even looked back on his past life, sometimes thought about his youthful verses as he had about other examples of youthful foolishness; but that he might be a poet was something he had long ago forgotten. He had become almost seventy years old. Life had slipped through his fingers—and not an hour, not a minute of the last three decades had been brightened by the knowledge of not belonging to the *others*. On the contrary—he had felt he belonged completely to those others. And they, too, all counted him as one of their own, while no one had the slightest inkling of who he really was! Only the young people of Vienna guessed at it—or indeed knew it to be true!

But where were they, these young people? A full three days had gone by since Wolfgang Meier's visit. What if he didn't come back?

It was a clear, not very cold winter's evening, and Saxberger went down onto the street; he had swallowed too much dust in his rummaging that afternoon. And gathering dust was all that those things would now do—at least on the face of it. But as he let the general impression the poems had made continue to act on him, he came to think that everything had stayed remarkably fresh, and that no small *joie de vivre* had flown up to him off those old pages. On reading one or other of the love poems there had even re-emerged, as if out of fog, some pale, sweet face which he had once seen, loved, kissed. Those pale, sweet faces! Where were they today? When he looked at the young girls who were walking past him, it seemed to him, as really it always did, that they were the same ones he had encountered there thirty and forty and fifty years ago. That they were the same ones he had kissed and whose—yes—whose praises he had sung.

He had reached the Ring at the point where many streets meet, where the Votive Church stands in airy grey, where the racket of all the carriages clatters together and great streams of people flow into one another. Suddenly he was standing in front of Herr Wolfgang Meier, who swept his hat off very low in front of him.

"What a delight," said Herr Meier, "to have such good luck. May I ask where your path leads?"

"I'm not heading anywhere in particular," replied Saxberger, who was very gladdened by this coincidence. "Just left the house to stroll around a little."

"Of course," said Meier, "you must really need that. If you're breathing in dust from those files all day…"

Saxberger wanted to retort that today's dust had not actually come from files, but he had the feeling that he himself should not join Meier in talking about these things.

"Would you allow me, my esteemed Herr Saxberger, if it wouldn't disturb you, to join your stroll?"

"Please do, it would be a pleasure."

"May I ask how you've spent the past few days?"

"Thank you, I've been very well. And what have you been doing? But yes! I still have to thank you for the poems you sent and for your kind inscription… I was very pleased, very pleased—" Saxberger had finished what he was saying, but Meier stayed silent, expecting to hear something about his poems. For the time being, Saxberger did not speak either. It did him good to have a young poet taking a walk by his side and waiting for his praise.

So the two of them carried on in silence for a whole half-minute, until Meier said: "And may I ask whether my modest verses were fortunate enough to meet with your approval?" His gaze deferentially sought Saxberger's.

The older man stopped walking and nodded.

"Certainly they met with my approval. Very fine I thought they were. Yes, I liked them very much."

"I hope," said Meier, "that your opinion isn't based on any charitable—"

"Oh no," interrupted Saxberger, becoming ever surer of himself as he carried on speaking, "I'm not being at all charitable; if I didn't like them, I would tell you straight out." He distinctly felt that he was gaining a greater and greater ascendancy over the younger man.

Meier said that he had started to write an epic and began to go into the details. An unease came over Saxberger. He was bored. He hardly listened to the young man, but when Meier paused he declared, "It's very interesting material, yes, you really must carry it through."

Meier thanked him for this encouragement and added: "If you only knew how much has been said about you at our table on recent evenings."

Saxberger's unease vanished at once. The young man had finally decided to go back to speaking about him. That was what had been missing. And, smiling comfortably, he asked:

"Well, what have you been saying about me? Did you give them my regards?"

"I did indeed. I also permitted myself to announce the existence of your play…"

"Oh, you really needn't have done that," said Saxberger, still smiling.

"You mean because it's been lost? I'm convinced that if you just think it over for a while, you'll definitely put your finger on where it can be found."

"Well, if you'd like to know: it already has been found."

"Ah!"

"Yes, it was lying in a drawer of my desk."

"And you had no idea?"

"Of course I had no idea. After all, it's been a long time since I was a writer!" And as he said that, he felt as if he were making a joke.

They had reached the Burgtor. Meier came to an abrupt halt and said, "Might I remind you of how you generously agreed to spend a little time with our circle? If you say yes, we can turn in here and go straight to the coffee house, where at this time of day we're sure to find some of my friends. Oh, please say yes! We would feel very honoured."

Saxberger believed that he had to make some objections. "Now?" he said. "But it must be almost eight." He looked at the clock. "Yes, it's already eight! That's when respectable people," he added with a smile, "are already—going to a restaurant."

"Oh, Herr Saxberger," countered Meier, "please don't brush my request aside. I think it's lovely that things today have come together so easily."

And soon they were heading across the Burgplatz towards the Old Town. Meier talked exuberantly and prepared Saxberger for the joyful surprise with which his friends would react to seeing him walk in with the poet of the *Wanderings*. Saxberger was excited. Entering a gathering where his presence represented a particular honour was something that had never happened to him before. When he arrived at his office, naturally his subordinates stood up—though that was only the politeness you had to show the boss. And at his usual communal table in the restaurant, he was no longer just some anonymous customer; sitting and having a drink together night after night had smoothed over certain differences in education that did undoubtedly exist between him and most of the others.

They stood at the door to the old Viennese coffee house. Saxberger knew it. He remembered that he had visited it from time to time in years gone by. Meier opened the door and let the elderly gentleman go in first. The low, vaulted room was quite full and the air was almost oppressively thick and smoky.

In a larger room to which the first one connected, people were playing billiards. Saxberger stopped briefly at the entrance to let his young companion go ahead. "Here they are," said Meier, and indicated a table by a recessed window not far from the door, where three young men were sitting.

"Good evening," said Meier. And, as he turned towards Saxberger, he introduced: "Herr Winder, Herr Christian, Herr *stud. phil.* Blink; Herr"—he paused—"Saxberger."

In that instant the young people's faces, which had until then been merely a little curious, transformed into expressions of happy satisfaction. They stood up and one, the pale little blond boy who had been introduced as Winder, moved his chair across for Saxberger and fetched himself another from a neighbouring table. When he had sat down, he gazed at the old gentleman in naïve admiration while the two others, friendly and slightly embarrassed, seemed to study the physiognomy of their new guest.

Meier continued: "Yes, I bring you the poet of the *Wanderings* and here, esteemed maestro, here you have the pride and hope of Young Vienna."

"It's a pleasure to meet you, gentlemen," said Saxberger. "It means I can thank you in person for the compliments you sent through your representative." And he glanced at Meier as if at an intimate friend of many years.

"It's a great honour to welcome you into our midst," said Blink.

"By giving you the names of these gentlemen, Herr Saxberger," said Meier, "I haven't told you very much. This man here"—and he gestured at Christian, who was very young and who, with his long hair, errant tie and somewhat unsteady eyes, most distinctly embodied the old stock figure of an "artist"—"he writes plays, mainly histories in five acts."

Christian interrupted. "They're not always in five acts, and they're not always histories. I write whatever the urge takes me to. It's just that it usually takes me to write history plays. I write what I *have* to. And that just tends to be history plays."

"My dear friend," said Meier, "that's exactly what I said. This man, on the other hand"—and he gestured at Blink, who was quite ugly and had a thin black beard and short-cropped hair—"is really more of a critic than a writer."

"I'm *solely* a critic," interjected Blink, who was still holding the newspaper in his hand and generally gave the impression that he would re-immerse himself in his reading as soon as there was something in the conversation he didn't like.

"Ah, you're a reviewer," said Saxberger, and looked upon him benevolently.

"Yes," Blink replied with force. "But I beg you not to confuse me with the other reviewers."

Saxberger, to whom, for various reasons, that idea had never occurred, was rather taken aback by this statement.

"And this gentleman," said Meier, indicating little Winder with a shrewd look, "this gentleman is a child and writes… everything."

"Ah," said Saxberger, laughing, and turned to this young person, who was sitting there very bashfully with one leg folded over the other and his hands crossed on his knee. "You write everything?"

"Yes," said Winder, and looked dazedly around the coffee house.

Just then there appeared at the door a very small, neglectfully dressed man who, as he saw someone unfamiliar sitting at the table, hesitated to come closer. But Meier noticed him at once and waved him over. "Come on," he said. The small man moved nearer with barely disguised mistrust.

"Albert Staufner, Herr Saxberger," said Meier. Staufner bowed curtly and said, as if he hadn't heard correctly, "Saxberger?"

"The poet of the *Wanderings*," Meier explained with some irritation.

"Aha!" said the small man, and nodded several times.

Then, still in his winter coat and with his hat still on his head, he sat down at the neighbouring table, but turned towards the others and said, "You know what?"

"Well?" they asked.

"I've been running around town all afternoon, I've been thinking about us, and something has to be done"—these phrases bubbled rapidly out of him.

"What has to be done?" asked Blink, who had put the newspaper down on his lap.

"People have to hear about us, people have to know about us. No one knows anything about us, not a soul bothers about us. The newspapers take no notice of us. Who's heard of Christian? No one! Who's heard of Meier? No one! Who's heard of Blink? No one! Who's heard of me? No one!"—Little Winder had expected to be named, too, and had become very uncomfortable at the prospect. He had almost been afraid. But now that he had been overlooked, he was put out after all.

"But how can anyone have heard of you?" said Meier. "You've never published anything."

"What use is publishing? Your poems are out at the moment—who gives a damn about them?"

"My 'Zenobia' should be published very soon," said Christian.

"And will anyone read it? No!" cried Staufner. "But it's not for nothing that I've spent all day rushing around. I've worked everything out. The whole programme. Because who but us is ever going to do anything to help? Who's ever heard of our 'Enthusiasm' society? We have to put something on. We have to put on readings."

"And who's ever going to go to them?" said Blink.

"You swine," shouted Staufner, springing to his feet.

Blink just laughed curtly. He seemed used to this kind of outburst. Saxberger was astounded.

"That's a stupid objection," continued Staufner, sitting down again. "And what'll ever get done if we go on like that among ourselves. Just take a look at *them*!" And he pointed at a table in the other corner of the room where, to Saxberger's surprise, no one was sitting.

"They understand how it works, they're promoting themselves! That one there"—and he pointed at an empty chair—"is about to have a play produced. And what are they? Nothing! All of them put together are nothing. They aren't people with ideals! Careerists is what they are, followers of literary fashion. No one pays any attention to what we do because we've struck out away from the beaten track and because we have ideals, something that's not appreciated nowadays. That's why I've drawn up a programme. I say all this in front of you, Herr Saxberger, because I know you are one of our own. You wrote the *Wanderings*, and the man who wrote the *Wanderings* is one of us."

Saxberger was completely dumbfounded by this unexpected turn in the conversation. Until then he had had the impression that this young man knew absolutely nothing about him.

He nodded and said, "Oh, don't worry. Please speak freely."

"Yes," exclaimed Staufner, "I can see that my words interest you. And I always say, if you want to drum up interest in an idea, you should go to the old people. The young ones see everyone who's coming up as just another new rival. I'll talk you through my programme and reflect on your advice, Herr Saxberger."

"But listen," responded the old gentleman, "I really don't think you're addressing yourself to the right person. I know so little about these things—yes, truly—I'm a quite uneducated person." He smiled at these words.

"I will permit myself to send you my 'Zenobia'," said Christian.

"What do we care about your 'Zenobia'?" cried Staufner.

"It wasn't to you that I promised it," Christian replied heatedly. Meier soothed them by saying: "Boys, boys!"

31

"We'll come to your plays later," said Staufner, a little more mildly, "but a lot later. I've already thought about it. We won't have any use for plays in our recital evening. It'll be a question of verse and of the novella. So…"

And he began to count up a list of names and to sketch out the programme.

Saxberger listened with interest. Around him was an atmosphere of hope, youth, self-confidence, and he breathed it in deeply. As the discussion became ever more impassioned, some of the words they were using began to sound familiar to him: words he had heard many years ago, perhaps even said himself, words he had thought of from time to time over the course of the passing years as if of something opaque or daydreamt, and which were now flying back and forth between these young people as if the words themselves had become young and alive once again. And it seemed to him that he belonged among these people. As if much of what they said of themselves was true also of him and as if he, too, still had battles to fight as they did. And as they, after a long to-and-fro, pressed his hand in parting and asked him to honour their group with his presence again as soon as he could, he declared that he had felt quite at home and would not fail to do just that. Outside the door they all said goodbye to the old gentleman and Meier offered to walk him some of the way home.

For a while they were both silent. Then Meier began: "May I ask, Herr Saxberger, how you liked it with us?"

"I liked it very much," replied Saxberger.

"Well," responded Meier, "it wasn't quite the proper thing tonight. And there were some people missing whom you would find very agreeable, like Friedinger, for example."

"Ah, you want to present something of his at your recital, don't you?"

"Yes. And then Bolling the actor, who is going to help out as well."

"Which theatre is he at?"

"None for the time being. Last winter he was in Abbazia… And then there's Fräulein Gasteiner."

"You mean there are women in your group?"

"Of course. She is a very remarkable person, you'll find her interesting. She has a wonderful voice."

"And where is she?"

"She's performed on various stages. But she's too eccentric, she doesn't fit into the regular theatre life."

Meier told him about some more members of his circle. Then, quite abruptly, he said, "And would you perhaps allow us to read something of yours as part of the recital?"

"Whatever do you need me for?" replied Saxberger. "You have such a rich selection already."

But Meier persisted and in the end Saxberger promised that he would pick out something well suited from among his works.

They said goodbye where they had encountered each other two hours before. Saxberger headed towards Währinger Straße and then to his habitual restaurant. As he entered, he was greeted no differently than usual; some took no notice at all of his arrival. Others called out a comfortable "*Servus*". As matter-of-course as that undoubtedly was, today he found it unseemly. And as he sat at his place and found himself surrounded only by mundane conversations in no way interrupted by his coming, he thought: you might have stood up when I walked in. But a quarter of an hour later, he was already caught up in the general discussion and had his opinion like all the others about the currency question, about the fraudster who'd been arrested the day before and about the unrest in Serbia.

* * *

Three evenings later, Saxberger was overcome by such a keen desire to see his young friends again that he curtailed his daily walk in the fresh air and found himself standing at the door of the coffee house as early as seven o'clock.

As he went in, he saw his acquaintances sitting at a larger table along with several people he didn't recognize. Meier came two paces forward to shake his hand and the other men rose from their seats. Those he didn't know were introduced to him. One was Friedinger, a fairly large and portly young person with a diminutive moustache; another was Bolling the actor, who had a malicious cut to his mouth; and the third was an already rather more mature man with a full black beard and a bald head, who was wearing a threadbare, double-breasted black frock coat. As this character, who went by the name of Linsmann, was introduced to Herr Saxberger, he took his hand, pressed it and nodded several times so seriously that it was as if he wanted to reassure him of his most heartfelt sympathies.

The conversation revolved around the recital evening. Staufner, who, as before, sat in his winter coat with his hat still on, had a sheet of paper on the table in front of him and was eagerly making notes. The programme was almost settled; except for Blink, who was solely a critic, and for little Winder, who wrote everything, who always sat there attentively and of whom no one took any notice, all those present were included in it. The bald gentleman with the black beard had been chosen to open the evening with a lecture titled "What we want". Saxberger learnt all this in the first fifteen minutes he was there. The bald man was to be helped in the composition of this lecture by the critic Blink.

"Gentlemen," said Blink, "if it's all right by Linsmann, I'll write the lecture myself, and Linsmann can read it, because he has such a sonorous voice."

To Saxberger's surprise, Linsmann nodded his agreement without appearing the least bit hurt.

Various other items on the programme were brought up. It was agreed that Bolling would also have to present something from an author who was already famous, in order to pre-empt the false assumption that the whole evening had been planned just to give publicity to a small clique.

"Gentlemen," said Staufner, "far be it from us to behave like that, and that's something Linsmann should emphasize in his speech, Blink."

"I know myself what Linsmann has to say," objected Blink. Linsmann stroked his beard and nodded.

"Oh!" cried Staufner, "that won't do! Each of us has the right to make proposals for the Linsmann speech. It's *our* programme that's supposed to be expressed in it, not the personal opinions of Linsmann."

Blink laughed. "I don't even know the personal opinions of Linsmann."

"And Herr Saxberger," Staufner suddenly said, "what's it to be for you?"

"Excuse me?" asked the man he'd addressed, a little abashed.

"You must read something! You're one of our own, so please do us the honour of standing up publicly as one of us."

"Yes, yes, yes," shouted the others.

Saxberger smiled, feeling moved, and replied: "Very flattering of you, but I can't give a reading. Really I can't. I've never had any kind of practice and, in any case, how would I fit in? You are all young people."

"You're young, too," said Meier very calmly, as though this were entirely self-evident.

"You're younger than we are," cried Staufner. "It's not a question of years, but of heart. The man who wrote the *Wanderings* must be a youngster."

"I was when I wrote it," countered Saxberger. "But that's quite a few years ago."

"That doesn't matter," said Staufner. "For today's generation, the *Wanderings* are the work of a newcomer—because no one knows them."

"And if Herr Saxberger," said Meier, "doesn't want to present an extract from his work himself, then Herr Bolling can read it instead."

"I'd be very glad to," said Bolling, who let them hear with his every word just what a good speaker he was.

"It looks to me," put in Herr Friedinger, "as if that lot over there are laughing at us." The others turned towards the table on which Friedinger had fixed his gaze, and Saxberger saw a group of five or six young people who seemed to be amusing themselves very highly.

"They wouldn't dream of it," cried Staufner, "they'll be laughing at some kind of hack joke."

"Who are those people?" asked Saxberger of Meier.

Christian, the tragedian, answered for him: "Those are the talentless ones."

"Is that known for a fact," Saxberger asked earnestly, "or do they call themselves that?"

"We call them that," mocked Friedinger. "And that one there"—he gestured at one of those sitting at the other table—"is about to have a play put on."

"Why do you call them talentless?" asked Saxberger, persevering.

"Talentless," interjected Meier in his calm way, "is what we generally call those who sit at different tables from us."

"Nonsense," shrieked Staufner, "they really are useless. Someone has to put them in their place."

"I'm writing an article about it," said Blink, his demeanour suggesting that this would dismiss them once and for all.

"Don't worry about them over there," said Staufner. "We were talking about Herr Saxberger taking part in our recital. And something else has occurred to me."

"Incredible," muttered Friedinger, but no one took any notice.

"Herr Saxberger," Staufner said to the old gentleman, "please write us something for our evening."

"But—?"

"Yes, write us something new. Our audience should be allowed to enjoy something of yours that's totally new, something completely unknown."

"Well," said Saxberger, "don't you think that the *Wanderings* are unknown enough?"

"They've been published!" argued Staufner. "Anyone can go out and buy them. How much greater would the interest be if, as part of our recital, you could get to hear a brand-new work by—Saxberger."

All the others agreed with Staufner's opinion, and Saxberger was pressed to please say yes.

"Gentlemen," he replied. "You must know that I have got quite out of the habit of writing poetry. No one ever paid any attention to me. That's not something that affects you at twenty-three; but, by and by... isn't that so, Herr Meier, we spoke about it just recently." Meier nodded and Winder gazed in silent admiration at the young man who had had such an intimate conversation with the old poet.

They began to talk about the ignorance and injustice of the public; that was something each of them had already experienced. Saxberger felt just how rough a ride the public had given him. He complained along with the others.

It had grown late, the company broke up. "You should write your memoirs," said Staufner, as he parted from the old gentleman.

When almost all of them had dispersed from the door of the coffee house, Saxberger found himself standing with Linsmann, who had barely said a word throughout the whole evening. And in Linsmann's face Saxberger again detected the expression of sympathy with which he had greeted him as he entered. "Yes," he said, and shook his head. "You, too, have been destroyed by the public."

Saxberger tried to rebuff him: "Destroyed... oh—"

"Of course," continued Linsmann. "It's been the same for you as for me. You know—they squashed me, just squashed me flat."

"Is that so?..."

"Well, and once someone's been squashed flat, what's he supposed to do? Do you really believe I could still bring anything off?"

"Oh..."

"Not a bit of it." He stared into the distance for a few seconds. Then he shook the old gentleman's hand, again with that understanding expression, and, smoking his Virginia cigar, slowly went on his way.

*   *   *

Saxberger became a diligent visitor to the coffee house. Every evening he arrived between six and seven o'clock, sat down at the table among his young friends and, although he didn't participate very actively in their conversations, he did listen attentively, even with relish. He almost felt that he was growing younger. A new era of his life seemed to have begun and from time to time he was a little disconcerted to think of the previous empty years, which now seemed very distant. After only a few days, he felt as at home among these young people as if he had known them for months. And they were right—he was one of them; he understood everything they said and he stood in the same relation to the rest of the world as they did: he had created something and sought the recognition that had been denied him. With them he had found it, at least in part, and done so at a time when he had almost forgotten he deserved it. He could no longer have any doubts about that and when, as sometimes happened, he leafed through his book of poetry, he himself lingered with a certain access of emotion over one or the other poem and began to shake his head in wonder at how the world could have passed so unheedingly over verses such as these.

And his young friends, too, spoke often about the ingratitude of the public. They, too, had, as they claimed, chosen their favourite poems from the *Wanderings*; and in a poem that Meier had written a few days earlier you could, in the others' estimation, clearly detect Saxberger's influence. After insistent pleading, Saxberger had also brought the publications that carried the poems not included in the *Wanderings*. The yellowed old pages went from hand to hand in the coffee house, and the young people went from one astonishment to another as they read the verses that would simply have been lost had it not been for the "Enthusiasm" society.

Little Winder asked Saxberger—it was the first time he had dared speak to him—if he could keep one of the old issues. Some of the young people decided to present him with manuscripts. He did not actually receive that many, because almost all of them were occupied with larger works that would be finished only over the course of the next few months. Nonetheless, Staufner gave him some poems that reminded him of Meier's, and from Friedinger he received some short stories that for reasons not immediately apparent to Saxberger he described as comic. Christian sent a five-act tragedy to his house... but Saxberger could never quite get down to reading the tiny, cramped handwriting.

They were soon ready to fix a date for the recital and to look around for a suitable venue in which to hold it. On the evening these questions were first discussed in earnest, and after their circle had already been together for some time, a woman entered the coffee house. She strode uninhibitedly, with a bright smile, to the table where the friends were sitting. "That's Gasteiner," Meier whispered to Saxberger.

"Hello, kids," she said as she reached them. "How are we all... Hello, Bolling," she added, and gave her hand to the actor, who was sitting in the middle of the others.

"Hello, Gasteiner," he replied.

"If you'll permit me," said Meier, and presented: "Herr Saxberger, the poet of the *Wanderings*—Fräulein Gasteiner, our tragedienne."

Saxberger stood and bowed to Fräulein Gasteiner. She was tall, no longer young, had a pallid face and wore dark make-up around her eyes. Her features were not unappealing and from a distance they even exhibited a kind of nobility which, however, disappeared up close. Then you saw the slightly crude shape of her mouth and the strangely ravaged lines of the face itself. Saxberger almost felt as if the woman who had appeared so imposingly at the door had, in sitting down beside him, become someone else entirely. She looked at the old gentleman with wide eyes. She rested her gaze on him for so long that he almost became embarrassed. Then she smiled and said, "So, you're an artist, too?!..."

"The poet of the *Wanderings*," repeated Meier with such force that the Fräulein turned and looked at him questioningly. The answer she read in Meier's eyes she understood so completely that she suddenly grasped her head, then clapped her hands together and, staring at Saxberger with even wider eyes than before, cried out: "The *Wanderings*?! You wrote the *Wanderings*?" And then, addressing herself to the others: "Yes, this—precisely *this* is how he would have to look."

"Herr Saxberger," said Christian, as he took the actress's strikingly long boa and hung it on a hook, "is going to take part in our evening."

"That's wonderful," exclaimed Gasteiner, and she again gave Saxberger her hand. Then, abruptly, she dropped out of this dramatic tone and back into the breezy one of before, saying, "Well, kids, what else is going on? Goodness, is that our little Winder [she had noticed him long before], how are you, little Winder?" Without waiting for an answer, she turned to the waiter. "Bring me whatever you want!"

"A café au lait?"

"For the love of God! Not a café au lait—an absinthe!" And, turning back to the others: "I would commit crimes for absinthe! I would murder for an absinthe. Now then, kids, who's coming on Sunday?"

"Where to, where to?" some of them asked.

"I'm giving a guest performance in the *Orphan* in Wiener Neustadt."

"You must be a splendid Jane Eyre," said Bolling. "Shame that Mr Rochester isn't in my line. I'd like to act opposite you in the *Orphan* sometime."

"We'll all go," said Staufner—"if only we could bring some of these measly Viennese theatre directors with us."

"I'm going, in any case," said Blink. "I'll see to it that there's something in one or two of the papers."

Fräulein Gasteiner pressed the critic's hand and shot him an ardent look. "I'll write to the director today so he can reserve some seats—one, two, three—"

"Not for me," little Winder said anxiously, "I don't think I'll come."

"Yes, yes, we already know," said Friedinger, "your mother won't allow it."

"Oh, I'm sure his mother will say yes," said Fräulein Gasteiner, looking tenderly at little Winder.

Bolling expressed the opinion that no modern actress anywhere would be able to play the "Orphan" after Gasteiner. The talk then turned to some of these actresses and Saxberger, like the others, was simply amazed by the incredible blindness of theatre directors, who always engaged the most talentless actresses around and let the best of them be poached not just by Berlin, Leipzig and Hamburg, but even by the theatres of Klagenfurt and Linz. Fräulein Gasteiner involved herself only very sparingly. She contented herself with giving an occasional melancholy nod or breathing a soft "Yes, that's how it is." And when the bitterness had risen to its high point, she spoke like a queen judging and pardoning: "Kids, let's leave off the poor little things [she meant the tragediennes of the Viennese theatre] and talk about your recital instead." With this word "kids", which Fräulein Gasteiner used so often, Saxberger felt he was being excluded.

"The things you've sent me are magnificent, truly magnificent!!"

Staufner handed her the sheet of paper which had of late always been on the table in front of him, and she quickly glanced over it.

"You, as you can see, are down for the third and sixth items."

She read in an undertone: "One… two… three… yes, there I am—right—four—Saxberger. So you yourself are going to read, Herr Saxberger?"

"Right," said Meier, "that's something we have to make a decision about. May I ask, Herr Saxberger, how things are with your new poem?"

Saxberger was both pleased and a little startled. Meier was talking about his new poem as though it were a matter of course. He hardly dared say that he hadn't even begun it yet. "You must leave me a little more time," he said in the end.

Fräulein Gasteiner suddenly burst out, "And may I present it?" She had trained her eyes on him as though this were a question of tremendous seriousness. Saxberger felt it: his answer had to be swift and decisive—this was a look that ordered and insisted. "I haven't even finished it," he replied. "I don't really know whether I'll—"

"If I don't have anything of yours to read, esteemed maestro—I'll cancel. I'll just cancel."

All of them began to assail him with pleas. It was under *his* aegis that they wanted to conquer. And he must promise, solemnly promise, that within a week at the latest, the new poem—it did not have to be particularly long—would be ready to be presented to their circle.

"Ah, we'll show that rabble," cried Staufner. "I know some people who're going to get the shock of their lives."

"Yes, kids, give it to them!" said Gasteiner.

"Keeping us hushed up was never going to work in the long term," added Friedinger.

Never yet had their spirits been so high and, as out of place as Saxberger had felt earlier that day, so well did he feel now. There was no doubt: it had been his promise that had animated the young people's hopes; the discussion turned around and on him; they looked up to him—he felt that he was their centre.

There was so much to discuss today that they decided to remain together past their usual time and all have supper in a restaurant. Saxberger was pressed to come with them. As they left the coffee house, he noticed to his surprise that the absinthe for which Fräulein Gasteiner would have committed crimes stood untouched on the table.

On the short way to the restaurant, Fräulein Gasteiner walked beside Saxberger. He could not but think how long it must have been since a woman had walked at his side. "I'm so happy," Fräulein Gasteiner said quietly, holding the end of the boa in front of her mouth, "that I'm to present your work." Then she asked him whether he had written much recently, which led him to talk again about his profession, about his office. Fräulein Gasteiner was deeply shocked.

"A civil servant—a man like you!" And she called Christian, who had been walking behind them, to come over.

"Do you hear that? This man, the poet of the *Wanderings*, is a civil servant—and you could have a position if you wanted but you won't accept it!"

Christian laughed mockingly and immediately dropped back again behind them.

"But where's the child?" Fräulein Gasteiner suddenly cried, looking around herself. Little Winder heard this shout and came running up from the rear. She took him by the hand and, catching hold of Saxberger's arm with her other, she said, "Listen, child, this is what you've got to make it to one day!"

Winder did not reply. But Saxberger saw that the young man was gazing reverently at him. And he said to the little one: "I hope you get further than I have!"

"Oh no, oh no," stammered Winder. And Fräulein Gasteiner smilingly stroked his cheek. Then she asked the old gentleman whether his job was a demanding one and why he did not give it up and instead devote himself unreservedly to his poetic vocation. And at all Saxberger's resigned answers there remained in Winder's eyes that same expression of sincerity and devotion.

"If I had had to choose any profession other than the theatre, I would have killed myself," said Fräulein Gasteiner.

Saxberger couldn't help thinking of the absinthe left in the coffee house.

They had reached the door of the restaurant. Meier played the guide, going ahead through the rows of tables to the smaller adjoining room, in which a long, narrow dining table offered enough space for all these guests. As they squeezed past the other tables, Linsmann happened to be next to Saxberger.

"Well, how do you like our tragedienne?" he asked.

"A very interesting person," responded Saxberger, in an unsettled, almost a questioning tone.

"Ten years ago," said Linsmann, "she even had a bit of talent."

They sat down casually around the long table. Fräulein Gasteiner had taken the seat on one side of Saxberger; on the other he had Meier.

Saxberger soon felt even more at ease here than where he usually ate, and the difference between the mundane conversations that were had there and the bold and cheerful talk that could be heard here impressed itself starkly upon him. And he spoke, too. He could already join in with them.

Fräulein Gasteiner sometimes tried to draw Herr Saxberger away from the general talk and into a private conversation. She spoke to him about her years as an "apprentice and journeyman", and seemed, to Saxberger's surprise, to believe she had made a career. Whenever she spoke to him her eyes were full of respect; sometimes tenderness flashed in them.

Suddenly, Staufner got up and began to give a toast. He started with some general remarks about art, touched on its coarsening in our times and eventually came to speak of the old masters who had held the banner of true art

aloft from their youth onwards and who, despite the indifference and indolence of the public, had serenely striven
towards their high and beautiful ideals. "One representative of these noble men, my friends, is among us today!
Never did he push himself forward; alone did he sit in his
cell, unworldly, scorning the world that didn't understand
him. But the people who do understand him have come,
they have made a pilgrimage to him, besought him to
place himself at their head and have said to him: you must
carry the flag, no one is worthier than you. [Bravo, bravo!]
You made the nation a gift of your artwork, and it paid
no heed. But we will tell the nation who you are, we will
force them to hear us! It is to the flag you hold aloft that
we make our oath. You are our teacher, our master, you.
We salute you, Eduard Saxberger!"

Their glasses rang against each other. Saxberger, proud
and confused, stood up with tears of feeling in his eyes,
and those sitting farther away came closer and clinked
their beer glasses against his. Fräulein Gasteiner let all the
others go first and only when the old gentleman had sat
back down, the noise and the chiming of glasses continu-
ing around him, did she take her spritzer and, looking
at him with damp eyes, lightly and gracefully touch her
glass to his. He felt very peculiar. At Staufner's opening

words he had been embarrassed, almost painfully moved. Over the course of the speech, however, this sensation had gradually fallen away. He believed himself to have heard the note of conviction in the speaker's words and, as the whole company was roused at the end and he was hailed as a teacher and master, his heart had been warmed so much that all his doubts were gently dissolved.

The acclaim of these youngsters felt to him like the belated fulfilment of many exhilarating things that he had fervently wished for many decades ago and that he had forgotten in his grey, everyday life.

He stood up to thank them. The loud gathering fell silent. It was a long time since he had spoken in front of such a large group. As a great quiet formed around him, he remembered the last occasion: when one of his subordinates had left the department and he had praised him warmly as the very exemplar of a conscientious civil servant. But how different... Suddenly there came to his lips the phrases with which the conscientious civil servant had answered him then. And he began...

"I'm so deeply touched that words fail me... really, gentlemen, I have no idea what I can say to you... you do me too much honour! [Oho!] I would very much like to express my gratitude—but you see, I have become an old man. [Oho!] The little that I've contributed [at this, the cries of 'Oho' became even stormier and Saxberger broke off the sentence]. My young friends," he continued, "there is nothing more pleasing to an old man [Oho!] than the recognition of the young. That it has been granted me in such a late year will always remain my greatest source of pride. And to this young generation, of which I have such outstanding representatives sitting around me now, to this young generation [and to his great relief, there came to mind all the refrains that he had recently heard so much of], which preserves the nation's aesthetic patrimony, which holds the banner of true art constantly aloft, to this young generation, to you, gentlemen, I raise my glass!"

And all at once it was over, actually against his will. He had wanted to say far more, a few words about each of his companions individually, but he had tumbled into his conclusion and could not get back out. Everyone again stood up. They drank his health, they thronged around him; Fräulein Gasteiner abruptly took his hand and pressed a kiss on it. No one settled back down. Conversations buzzed over and across each other.

Linsmann, who had had a lot to drink, was speaking in emphatic tones to Blink the critic and putting forward some ideas of his own for the recital evening's introductory speech. Little Winder was leaning against the wall and had the feeling that he was present at a momentous occasion. Staufner, who was in a state of the highest excitement, was standing with Bolling behind old Saxberger's chair and giving impassioned voice to his indignation about a great range of things and people.

Christian, the composer of tragedies, had pulled a seat up next to Fräulein Gasteiner and was talking to her so closely that his lips almost grazed her neck. Friedinger was sitting broadly on two chairs, staring a little stupidly into the middle distance. Meier was standing next to him and was the calmest of them all.

"Do you know what I'm curious about?" he said to Friedinger.

"What?"

"How the new work from the old gentleman will turn out." And he smiled at these words. It was not clear to Friedinger whether this was friendly curiosity or mocking scepticism.

Friedinger, who always became exceptionally earnest when he had been drinking, replied: "The old man, he's a genius! He's an unrecognized genius!" He was almost in tears.

"Indubitably," responded Meier...

It was past midnight when they thought of leaving. Saxberger did not feel the least bit tired. He could have sat there until the early morning, listening to the young people and chatting with them. When he stood up, Fräulein Gasteiner, despite his protests, helped him with his winter coat and, as he took his scarf from the pocket, would not be prevented from wrapping it round his neck herself and arranging it into very dainty folds.

When the company went out onto the street, a mild blue night hung over the city. After the stifling, eye-burning fug of the restaurant, the cool, soft air came as a blessing. It seemed that the weather had turned while they had been sitting in there, and Fräulein Gasteiner cried, "Springtide has come!"

As Saxberger tried to say goodbye, it became apparent that no one was thinking of going home. And so they all walked the old gentleman back to his apartment.

On his right strode Fräulein Gasteiner, who from time to time dropped back with some other member of their group but always returned to Saxberger's side, as if to her rightful place. The whole company was in constant, restless movement. On the dark and quiet Burgplatz, across which their route took them, Friedinger the humorist began to weep. Saxberger worriedly asked what this meant, but received the reassuring explanation that it always happened after they'd been carousing. On the Ringstraße, Linsmann, the bald, squashed Linsmann, abruptly began to whistle loudly. To Saxberger's amazement, the boisterous conversation among the others went silent and everyone listened. Saxberger learnt that Linsmann had achieved an astonishing virtuosity in the art of whistling, but unfortunately only rarely condescended to give a demonstration of his skill.

He whistled several Offenbach melodies and stopped completely unexpectedly, halfway through an arietta, with the cry: "Miserable mob!"

In response to a questioning look of Saxberger's, Meier, who was walking next to him, explained: "He means the French."

"Herr Linsmann," called Fräulein Gasteiner, "you whistle like a god!"

The old gentleman felt light and happy. And he thought: why all this only now? It's so late! If only this had happened to him thirty—or twenty, oh, if only it had happened five years ago! But then his sense of his own freshness and youthfulness again came upon him so strongly that he had to say to himself: it is not too late.

And he involuntarily thought of the phrases with which this evening would necessarily have been described by someone who hadn't been there. Proud words appeared in him: they accompanied him home in triumph—in triumph… accompanied the poet… And he delighted in how the young people came to his side one after another, how each strove to snatch a few words with him, how each tried to make himself as agreeable as possible to him. And he delighted in how unassumingly he could tell them about himself, about the disappointments of his youth, about his silent, lonely existence, about living in the modest apartment with its view of the hills in the nearby Wienerwald. And the admiring, even tender glances from Fräulein Gasteiner also did him good, and when Staufner at one point whispered to him, "Take a look at Christian, he's jealous," he had to smile.

When he reached the door of his building and pulled the bell, they all waited until the concierge came to open up and, as he stepped through the entrance, they shouted: Hurrah! hurrah! hurrah! And the bewildered face of the concierge was a pleasure, too. The old gentleman took the small lamp with the candle and slowly climbed the stairs. The confusion of voices still sounded in his ears. Now that he was quite alone and his steps resounded in the stairwell, the evening that had just passed seemed to have been wondrous and strange.

As he walked into his room, he, as usual, put the light down on the little bedside table. Then he stepped across to the window. He still had the voices in his ears. No, no—he was hearing them, he was hearing them really. And indeed—they were still standing down there, down outside the door. All of them who had accompanied him home.

He hurriedly opened the window and leant out. They had doubtless expected he would show himself because, as soon as his head appeared, the noise of their cheers rang up to him again: Hurrah! hurrah! hurrah! He bowed. They shouted "hurrah" a few more times, he called out a heartfelt "goodnight", and they unhurriedly set off for home.

He saw them wandering away down the street; he followed them with his eyes until they disappeared around the corner. Then it was quiet in the alley. There was no one anywhere in sight. Only then did the old gentleman notice that it had grown a little chilly in his room. He quickly closed the window and moved away from it. He sat on his bedside chair and shook his head. He was touched. The light of the candle on the table stretched oddly upwards and shimmered fuzzily—there were tears in his eyes.

*   *   *

On the following afternoon, Saxberger sat down at his desk, reclined in his chair and considered. Today he had to make a start on the poem for the recital. One thing he was sure of: that he would have been as good as unable to choose any topic other than the unfamiliar feelings the recent weeks had brought him. What else would he have had to say? Should he just invent something from scratch? He could have floundered around like that for a long time. He felt very definitely that the time for that was over.

So there was no need to give any more thought to the selection of material. But as he tried to grasp it, as he began to search for phrases with which to express it, he noticed to his surprise that, while he sat there quietly, nothing occurred to him. He stood up, he paced up and down the room, he mumbled to himself. He tried to snatch at the individual words, which would not stand still but which, hardly had they appeared, seemed to vanish again as if into mist. He had to say them out loud to himself so as not to keep losing them again... An old man... forgotten... forgotten... lying in a dream... dreamt... I've awoken... forgotten... dreamt...

He made no progress. It was as if his thoughts were blocking each other; all at once he no longer knew what he was thinking about. He went over to the window and looked into the distance, into the grey skies. And he began again.

Forgotten… then the young generation came… they brought me the wreath…

No, no, that wouldn't do at all. That bit about the wreath was ludicrous.

And he asked himself: so, what did the young people do?… the young… they came, they bent their knee… and the old man awoke… he awoke from a dream… I was dreaming… I dreamt my life… yes, that was good, it had to be taken on from there: that he had actually dreamt his life. But how to go on?… Always the same words again… a dreamt life, a dreamt life… and he could not get past them. It was as if someone were holding him fast on these few syllables, the way you press someone down into an armchair. He rubbed his forehead, he again started to pace up and down the room, that was better. Albeit that nothing else came to him. But his frustration was alleviated by the movement. Movement! Yes… out onto the streets… into the fresh air! After all, he must remember that he had not slept very much, his head must be clouded.

He took his hat and stick and he went. For half an hour at least he wanted to suppress any attempt at further thought, so as then to start anew and afresh. But this was most peculiar: the phrases continued to whirr in his ears as he went down the stairs and then still when he was on the street; and as he tried to divert himself by reading the names on signs or observing the people going past—it didn't help. Again and again it whirred in his brain: …I have dreamt my life… and the words didn't even mean anything any more. They were only sounds, and he did not even quite understand them. Suddenly he said to himself: enough is enough. He had said it out loud. And it sounded so energetic that it was as though someone else had called to him. He sighed as if a curse had been lifted.

Honestly, what had he been thinking of, choosing today of all days—when he wasn't in the mood, when he was tired and worn—to slog through the composition of a poem? He made a firm resolution not to think any more about it for the rest of the day. The whole day would be devoted to recovery. And with that he felt well again. Nor did he have any doubts that tomorrow or the day after he would achieve with ease what today he had struggled for with so much effort, and in vain. He decided not to go and see his young friends this evening. He feared the fug and the noise. And there was something else that held him back, something that had already crossed his mind once or twice in the previous days: he wanted to make himself a bit scarcer.

He would spend a quick hour in a little coffee house near his apartment that he sometimes frequented.

He went there, sat by a window, had himself brought a café au lait and watched with interest as a game of billiards was played by several old gentlemen. Two of these were well known to him. They belonged to the same table as him at his usual restaurant and, when he came in, had greeted him with a very loud "*Servus*", which to him seemed so horribly unfitting that he was almost put out of sorts. But after he had sat for a few minutes at the small table, he began to feel so at home that he did not even take the request that he keep score at all badly, and followed the game with keen attention.

An extremely interesting shot was played and the game shifted into a whole new phase. From this moment on, Herr Saxberger was completely absorbed. He butted in, he gave advice, he took sides, he even offered to take a difficult shot for one of the men, something that was sarcastically declined. Saxberger was almost insulted by that and very pleased when the mocker's shot went so wrong that it lost him the game.

When it was finished, he went with his two acquaintances to their restaurant. One of them was a retired major, the other the proprietor of a large delicatessen.

In the restaurant they took their places at their usual table, where around ten men were sitting. One was having his name day and had ordered several bottles of wine to celebrate. The conversation was loud and lively; Saxberger sometimes joined in. From time to time it seemed bizarre to him that they spoke to him as to one of their equals. But indeed—what did they know of him! What could they know of him! By what had he ever given them to understand that he was of a different sort than they.

Herr Grossinger, the delicatessen owner, who was considered the company's wittiest soul, stood up and delivered a toast in verse. It was harmless rhyming doggerel with a few jokes aimed at the predilections of the man being celebrated—at his preference for particular dishes, at a tender inclination he was said to feel for a female tobacconist, at a bright-yellow raincoat that he liked to wear even in the finest weather. While these verses were being greeted with hearty laughter, Saxberger sat there smiling genially. He thought to himself: would they dare present this "poem" if they knew who I am? He took a distinct pleasure in being able to attend this party, as it were, incognito, and when Herr Grossinger finished his toast to general applause, he clapped along with the rest.

"Splendid, splendid… Grossinger's done very well there—so he can write poetry, too—he's a hell of a man, that Grossinger," was what they were all saying over each other. Saxberger shook the delicatessen owner's hand and said: "Very nice."

"Well, I ask you," said the major, "that was no run-of-the-mill occasional poem, you really have to say that was something more, true poetry…"

Saxberger looked at the major, quite nonplussed. Some of the others voiced their agreement.

"You could have that published, just the way it is! Splendid! I always say it, old Grossinger!"

Saxberger had an unpleasant feeling: he would have liked to make a critical comment, because he had not enjoyed the poem. The verses he had found stale, the rhymes forced. He was slightly angered by the self-satisfied face of the delicatessen owner and by the excessive praise that was being showered upon him.

But he stayed silent. He felt very clearly that any word of criticism coming now would spoil the group's good mood. Also, it would have been taken in the wrong spirit, and so he remained sitting quietly.

Soon another of the company stood up and toasted the man whose name day it was. He was a schoolmaster and, in a few earnest words, he portrayed the man as the model of all civic virtues. Soon after him yet another stood up and drank the health of "the ladies".

Again they applauded, again they congratulated the speaker; Grossinger's fame had faded. But still it gnawed at Saxberger. He was overcome by an irresistible urge to tell them about himself, to remove his mask. He wanted to leap to his feet and suddenly shout to them all: I am a poet. He wished there had been someone there to tell them all the story of his life… But it wasn't as if he had to say straight out: "I am a poet"; there were ways of dropping a gentle hint. He stood up and went into the corner of the room, where his overcoat was hanging. He took a cigar from it and then stopped behind Grossinger. "Very good! Should I… give you my works as an encouragement?"

Grossinger turned around. "What works are those?"

Saxberger lit his cigar with feigned equanimity. "You see, I can write poetry, too," he said.

"Really?" said Grossinger and turned back around.

Saxberger did not think that was at all proper. He saw that these kinds of generally couched remarks would not have any effect and, putting his hand on the delicatessen owner's shoulder, he said, almost bitterly:

"I wrote a whole book of poetry when I was a young man, you understand?"

Grossinger looked blankly at the old gentleman, then turned, smiling, to the man being celebrated, who was sitting beside him, and said:

"D'you hear what Saxberger's been saying? He's written a whole book of poetry." The man smiled contently, without even looking around. "God will forgive him," he said.

Saxberger sensed that there was no going back and said: "You don't understand what I mean! I wrote a book—it was published, you understand?"

"Well," cried Grossinger, "then you were wickeder in your youth than most! Imagine sending it straight to the printers!"

Saxberger was furious. "I didn't write doggerel! Verse, beautiful, long, serious things are what I wrote, you understand?" Saxberger had started to speak so loudly that it caught the attention of some of those sitting nearby.

Grossinger laughed and said to Saxberger: "Why are you telling us this? If you'd never written any poems, that would be much stranger!"

And before Saxberger could make a comeback, some of the others involved themselves in the conversation. It turned out that each of them had written poems at one time, and they laughed as they remembered it.

Saxberger, who had stayed behind Grossinger's chair, could not listen to this for long. His bitterness melted away. He felt scorn and pity for these people… He—had to remain incognito; they took his mask for his true face. Something inside told him that even if he were to read them his works, they would not know more of him than before. They considered anyone who happened to end up among them to be a person like them. What could you do…

Saxberger took his coat from the peg, and went. It wasn't noticed. The group were still talking and shouting over one another. As the old gentleman stood outside on the street, he started to feel uncomfortable. No—he did not want to come here again, at least not in the near future. What he would have most liked to do was go straight to his young friends, to hear from them again that he did not belong to those others, and that he was indeed a poet!

The next evening, Herr Eduard Saxberger again made his way to the coffee house to join his young friends and received in deep satisfaction the respectful greetings with which he was welcomed. Fräulein Gasteiner, too, was present and, as she reached out her hand to him, a smile played across her lips as though she were greeting an old, dear friend.

"So today we've announced ourselves," said Meier, passing him a newspaper and pointing to the notices. Saxberger read: "Club news—the literary society 'Enthusiasm' will soon be putting on an evening of recitals. Among others, the venerable poet Saxberger has kindly agreed to take part."

Saxberger did not immediately put the newspaper down, but acted as if there were more he still wanted to read. In truth, the announcement had made such a strong impression on him that he had to hide how affected he was… the venerable poet Saxberger… What he thought of above all were the men from the Pickled Pear and especially of Herr Grossinger. Then he thought of the many other people who had never heard of him and would today be asking themselves—why don't we know this name?

It didn't say… Herr Saxberger—not the civil servant Herr Saxberger—no, "the venerable poet Saxberger"—that was who he was, he himself. And none of those present made any kind of reference to this epithet. They obviously considered it entirely self-evident.

If only he had met them sooner! Then he would not have given up so quickly, nor mixed with the quotidian rabble that didn't understand him.

The loud chatter around him roused him from his thoughts. Staufner was telling them that he was often incapable of writing verse for weeks at a time, but that there were specific places which had a revivifying effect on his eagerness to work. Which places these were he did not want to reveal.

"Maybe it's superstitious, but I think that if I told anyone, the magic would vanish."

Much was now said about this. Christian explained that the idea for each of his dramas had occurred to him in Sievering and that he wrote his best scenes when lying on his back in the grass.

"I have an idiosyncrasy," said Bolling the actor, "that really is odd: I always study best if I keep my desk drawer full of lots of rotten… bitter oranges."

"Have you always preserved them?" asked Blink.

Bolling was about to object to this remark. But he remembered that Blink was a critic and laughed good-naturedly.

"Well, what kind of mood do you need?" Meier asked of little Winder.

"I," he replied, reddening... "I can actually always write..."

"Always!" laughed the others.

Winder looked around for help. His gaze came to rest on Saxberger, who regarded him kindly.

The conversation continued. As soon as Staufner had mentioned this peculiarity, that he was able to compose only in specific places, a memory had struck the old gentleman. He remembered all at once where, in his day, his best thoughts had sprung to mind. He remembered how as a young man he had often strolled along the bank of the Danube canal at twilight, along the brown footpath that leads to Nussdorf... It was there, he suddenly knew, that his best verses had always come to him.

And as the talk again turned to the programme and Staufner asked whether they could yet be told the title of the new work he was preparing for the recital, he smiled and said: "'Evening Moods' is what it'll be called."

That day, too, he went to the restaurant with the young people and felt very much at his ease among them. Fräulein Gasteiner again sat beside him and was far more charming even than on the previous occasion. She was interested in the most insignificant details of how he lived. She asked about how he divided up his day; she wanted to know how his room was arranged; she showed a matronly understanding of all the trifling elements of running a household. That did not at all fit with the picture that he had had of her. And at one point he said to her in great surprise: "I had no idea you would understand these things so well."

"Two souls, alas," she replied, "dwell within my breast… Of course I'm an artist and I'm devoted to my art with every fibre of my heart, but sometimes I long for peace, for hush, for…"

She broke off.

"For what?" asked Saxberger.

She lowered her eyes and was silent. And as she suddenly lifted them again, she said decisively: "Let's leave it… it's all right… I belong to art. No one"—she repeated the word, giving Herr Saxberger a look that was almost stern—"*no one* will succeed in tearing me from it."

Although she had previously been speaking quite quietly, with these words she raised her voice so that those sitting nearest them could hear her.

And that evening, too, as it approached midnight, toasts were made, mainly to the imminent recital and to art in general. On the way home, Saxberger was again accompanied by the whole party.

"Listen," said Linsmann, "Gasteiner is carrying on with Christian."

Saxberger looked at Linsmann. "What… does that have to do with me?"

"I just thought you didn't know… Oh yes, she's a fine one…"

"How do you mean that?"

"Oh, women, women—" He said nothing for a while, then added in lachrymose tones: "D'you have any inkling how utterly I fell for it?" and didn't say another word.

When Linsmann had rejoined the others, Fräulein Gasteiner came over to the old gentleman's side. "I know what Herr Linsmann whispered to you," she said simply.

Saxberger stayed silent, in some embarrassment.

"He told you," continued Fräulein Gasteiner, "that the gentleman with the long black hair is my lover."

"But…"

Fräulein Gasteiner smiled disdainfully. "I have never yet been able to have a friendly association with a man without it being said that he is my lover."

"But that's…"

"Oh, it's been a long time since I bothered about it, but I also know what Herr Linsmann didn't tell you."

"Yes?"

"That he once went flying down some stairs because he dared step too close to a certain lady."

"Ah…"

"I forgave him for it long ago. But the one thing that repels me about that person is his need for revenge…"

Just then, the vengeful Linsmann again began to whistle and, just as the last time, the group grew quiet and listened. Later, when they were already on the Währinger Straße, Friedinger leant against a lamp post and contributed his own regular number by beginning to sob. Today, however, he was paid no attention whatsoever and soon calmed down.

When they reached Saxberger's house, they all waited until the concierge came to open up. Saxberger went quite quickly up the stairs and, when he reached his room, hurried to the window. He saw the whole company just disappearing around the corner. They hadn't waited this time for him to reappear. He was a little disappointed. Also, Linsmann's comments had left an unpleasant aftertaste.

Nonetheless, it was not hard to understand why Herr Linsmann had had his head turned by Fräulein Gasteiner. Twenty years ago she would have appealed to him, too, but today… And he had to smile wryly as the notice about the "venerable poet" again occurred to him.

There followed days of rain. Saxberger had to postpone his walk from evening to evening, and on evening after evening he sat in the coffee house with his young friends. The trim old gentleman with the proper, slightly old-fashioned suit and the smooth-shaven, good-natured face had long since been noticed by the coffee house's regulars, and become a familiar figure. Sometimes he even believed himself to have overheard people at neighbouring tables asking after him. At first, being noted in this way had been slightly embarrassing, but he soon grew used to it. Their circle was practically always there in full, and even Fräulein Gasteiner came almost predictably. Her guest performance had been temporarily put back. It seemed that the incumbent lead at Wiener Neustadt had intrigued scandalously against her.

The recital came ever closer and Saxberger had not written a line of his "Evening Moods". Late one mild afternoon, he decided finally to take his stroll along the Donaulände.

It was still bright when he reached the Augarten Bridge.

He thought of how often in the last years he must have seen the path that ran below where he was standing and then along the canal towards Nussdorf, between the lumber yards and the unhurried grey river—and always without ever remembering the days of his youth. In that instant it was incomprehensible to him how many profound interior experiences were extinguished by the mere wretched flow of existence as if they had never been. It also struck him that sometimes he had not gone that way alone. He no longer knew with whom. He could not remember any particular person, and that gave his reminiscing an especial melancholy.

He walked slowly down the broad, gently descending path that begins right beside the bridge and continues on flat and evenly. The nearby hills that reared up almost over him were already blurring at their edges and the twilit sky had lowered itself deep down onto them. On the canal, a long boat was moving upstream, pulled by horses which went their heavy, tired way along the bank. On the other side of the canal stood the high white and yellow houses of the Brigittenau, which became ever barer and drearier the closer they came to the edge of the city. A great number of tall factory smokestacks stretched above them into the sky. On this bank, the prospect was tightly hemmed in. The path led past lumber yards, and the logs and beams were stacked so high that they blocked the view almost completely. Only between the individual planked-in yards did tight paths lead out and again flow into the broader streets.

He encountered few people. Some pairs of lovers, a few customs officials, women leading their children by the hand. On the bank sat a number of miserably dressed people. A couple caught the old gentleman's eye: she, a very young thing in a little blue linen dress, with no hat but a headscarf that had slid down and whose ends hung round the nape of her neck; he, a very tall, sick-looking young man with a pale, beardless face. He saw these two coming towards him from far off; it was as if they were floating forward out of the gloom. They weren't talking, they stared in front of themselves, some unspeakable sadness lay in their tread. And Saxberger was compelled to turn around after they had passed him to see them go walking silently on, still with that sad, floating tread, until they disappeared in the gloaming...

All the human noises he could hear came from the other bank. They reached him just as they were dying away. From that other side he also heard the whistling of locomotives and the distant groaning of the steam trams. Then he heard a shout from beside him. The coachman trotting along with the horses hauling the boat was driving the animals on. Saxberger stood aside for a few minutes to let them pass; only then did he realize he had been walking beside them for all this time… And as he stood still, he suddenly felt very alone. It was as if everything living was receding from him. Even the light of day seemed to be sneaking away more hastily than before and, when he looked in the direction of the hills, they had vanished completely. The night lay upon them.

All this was observed by Saxberger. He could not close his senses to these outer things, as little as they meant to him. Minutes and quarters of an hour went by. As the deeper dusk descended, the reason he had come here again weighed heavily upon him. He had wanted to think about his poem, yes, to think. Phrases, verses were what he was here to look for.

He stopped, he even closed his eyes. But then all the noises grew louder; noises that he hadn't even noticed before entered his mind. He heard carriages rolling over the bridge nearby, he heard the horses' hooves striking the escarpment, he heard the waves quietly, very quietly lapping the banks. He opened his eyes; it seemed to grow stiller. Lights were beginning to glow on the other side.

The lanterns on the opposite street were being lit one after the other and he felt somehow forced to watch each lamp come on after the last.

Lights were also appearing on the distant railway bridge, with an intensely red one right in the middle. He didn't understand why he was watching all this so attentively, but he couldn't turn away. It was impossible for him to settle to quiet contemplation… it was as if the few poor thoughts he had already caught were fluttering off again. Only one dead, incomprehensible word remained and buzzed in his head… evening… evening…

Now the bells sounded from their towers; three or four rang out at once. They seemed to make such a loud noise that all other sounds were swallowed up by it.

It was dark and the old gentleman decided to turn around. He walked quite rapidly. He had a yearning for the bright, inhabited streets. He knew now: his efforts were in vain. Laughable was what they had been. It was over. At heart it was simple and not even very sad—no sadder than age itself, hardly sadder than the thirty years in which no verse had ever occurred to him.

But that wasn't even the crux of it. He also knew that everything would have been different if his outer life had turned out differently, if the public had taken notice of him then. There was no doubt that that would still have had some significance for how he himself had turned out; back then, it would not have been merely a pleasure, it would have been a stimulus—the soil had been fresh and moist…

Now his soul was… a dry, frozen clod… he couldn't help but smile: he was thinking in images, as if he really were a venerable poet…

He had got back to the Ring and all the clamour of the city was again about him. He was not really in the mood to go to the coffee house, today he just wanted to go home for once, sit himself down comfortably in his easy chair, read something, something very light, and not go back out onto the street. To his surprise, he was hardly discountenanced. Indeed, he was pleased that he definitely did not have to write anything. The idea of doing so had made him uneasy from the start—now he had been excused it and he was almost happy.

When he arrived home, he found a letter that a porter had brought over. The handwriting on the envelope was not familiar. He opened it. The script was large and had long, fine strokes. He turned the sheet over, the signature read: Ludwiga Gasteiner.

What did she want? He read the letter.

"Maestro! Today I read the *Wanderings*. Don't ask for the how manyth time. I don't know. You are a great artist. I need to tell you how much I admire you. I never find the right words, esteemed maestro, when I am fortunate enough to be with you. But I *must* tell you, today, after a sleepless, tormented night, in which I, for the third time, read your *Wanderings* straight through! Your Ludwiga Gasteiner."

The date was missing, but the address, IX, Severingasse 77, was given. Saxberger laid the letter down on the desk and thought. It had been years upon years since any kind of woman had turned her attention to him, and long since he had even regretted it... but now it was all coming at once...

He imagined Fräulein Gasteiner coming into the room, ardently kissing his hands, as she already had once before, and crying tears on them. He knew it would do him a lot of good.

*   *   *

The next day, when Herr Saxberger entered the coffee house, the members of "Enthusiasm" were already gathered there. Fräulein Gasteiner was there, too, and, as Herr Saxberger sat down, she gave him her hand with a smile in her eyes, which she immediately cast down again as if something very sweet and secret had happened between them.

On the table lay several printed sheets. It was the final programme for the recital. Saxberger took one—he found his name and, with a mild fright, read: 3. Eduard Saxberger, "Evening Moods"… Fräulein Ludwiga Gasteiner.

He wanted to say something at once, but didn't quite dare. It was highly embarrassing. They were having a very heated discussion about Linsmann's speech, which Blink had presented in outline before Saxberger's arrival. Meier felt that, taken as a whole, it was too much of a polemic.

"Coward," muttered Staufner.

"You're mistaken," replied Meier, very calmly. "I just don't think it's necessary to attack a whole heap of people who've never done anything against us."

Most of the group seemed sympathetic to Meier's viewpoint. But when the question already seemed to have been settled, Linsmann suddenly interjected: "No," he shouted, "I won't let you ruin my speech. Not when I can finally tell people what I really think—I've got no pity for them; they've never had any for me."

They soothed him. They explained to him that he, as the one giving the speech, could put into his tone all the hatred deserved by the people who "had never had any pity for him". In fact, that would make an even stronger impression. Eventually he was satisfied. They saw that he was, even though he kept repeating: those people need to be told for once—they have to be told!

As they then reached the third item, a slightly disgruntled Staufner turned to Saxberger as if it were a matter of something purely incidental. "You've already given Fräulein Gasteiner the 'Evening Moods'?"

"No," replied Saxberger.

Staufner's forehead drew up into slight wrinkles. "And when…" he asked.

"Gentlemen," said Saxberger, and he smiled a little shamefacedly. "I have to admit something…"

Everyone looked at him expectantly, making him very uncomfortable.

"You see, I have—I've been a bit… lazy, yes, it's true, I haven't done anything, anything at all! Yes, just look at me"—he laughed in his embarrassment—and suddenly said very vehemently: "I haven't written a line! Well, and what are you going to do to me?"

They were silent. It was far more painful than Saxberger had imagined. They seemed very disappointed. Meier said, "That's a shame, a real shame."

"So, what are we going to do?" said Staufner.

"You'll just have to inform the press," said Saxberger, who felt a need to bring as much jocularity as possible into the conversation. "One of those notices... the... venerable poet has stood us up..."

"Please," said little Winder, and was so self-conscious that the word came out too loud, "...please... there are already so many beautiful things by Herr Saxberger, thank God, that we..."

He looked around the coffee house and said no more.

"That's true," said Staufner, "we do have the *Wanderings*..."

"The *Wanderings*..." whispered Fräulein Gasteiner, who cast a shy glance at Herr Saxberger and then looked dreamily into nowhere.

"Are you in agreement," Staufner turned (almost) sternly to Herr Saxberger, "that Fräulein Gasteiner will present something from the *Wanderings*?"

"With pleasure," replied Saxberger.

When Fräulein Gasteiner heard his voice she looked up again, as if awaking from a distant reverie.

"All right," said Staufner—"so that's that taken care of... but what are we going to do about the programme? It's already there in print, 'Evening Moods'."

"That doesn't matter," objected Meier in his calm way, "we'll just choose poems—or perhaps Herr Saxberger will choose poems that *could* be called that… it won't be very difficult. Ultimately, all lyrical poems are either morning moods or evening moods…"

"Or night moods," added Friedinger as forcefully as if this joke were of the utmost importance.

Fräulein Gasteiner spoke up: "Let me choose the poems," she said.

"As Herr Saxberger wishes," said Staufner, somewhat unwillingly, and passed straight on to the fourth item in the programme.

Saxberger was no longer really listening. He could feel that his admission had gone down badly. This was something they hadn't expected, that he would ultimately be too "lazy" to do it. At heart, they even considered it ingratitude—in a sense. It had been *they* who'd discovered him after all this time. They had rallied around him. They professed themselves to be in some regard his pupils. They publicized his name—and now, when he was supposed to do them this one favour, he was—too lazy… too lazy? But why too lazy! It had only been an excuse and a very stupid one at that—he had been in good faith, he had sat there for hours at a time and thought. Just yesterday, he had traipsed along the Danube and racked his brains—it was just that nothing had occurred to him, or: he hadn't found the right atmosphere!

Why hadn't he said that? No one could have blamed him for that; everyone would have understood—more than that: they would perhaps have felt sympathetically moved. What could have prompted him to tell them something false that also sounded so much more unfavourable than the truth? He worried at himself until he was almost sick. He felt as if his position in the circle had been shattered. He continued to eat away at himself even when the young people had long ceased to think of it and were talking through the other items on the programme. Even the damp, lingering gazes that Fräulein Gasteiner occasionally aimed at him couldn't bring him out of his bad mood.

And when there was a pause in the discussion, he abruptly began to speak without having decided to do so beforehand and, as if nothing else had been spoken about for all this time and he were simply carrying on, he said:

"Well, it wasn't laziness, you mustn't think that I was happy to let you down, gentlemen. It's just, when you've been away from it all for so long—when you've become an old man—then it's not so easy any more to get into the right frame of mind."

"Of course, of course," murmured Meier and Blink but, overall, very little notice was taken of what the old gentleman had said. It seemed to be all the same to them whether it was out of laziness or a lack of the right mood that he hadn't got anything together.

As they left the coffee house, Linsmann amiably and without further ado hooked his arm through Saxberger's, which he never had before, but sometimes did when walking along with Friedinger or one of the other disciples. It made Saxberger feel strange. We're not really such good friends, he thought. And it struck him: however things panned out—he, Saxberger, was nonetheless, even if he never wrote another line, a man with a profession, he was what was more or less justly called a useful member of human society. But Linsmann, if he didn't write anything else—and he had stopped writing long ago—was nothing, nothing at all—a "squashed man", as he had said himself, one who could do nothing but rant and borrow money from everyone, even from little Winder. And this Herr Linsmann was now collegially walking arm in arm with him.

"Shall I tell you something, Herr Saxberger?" he said. "I have prospects! I have prospects!"

Saxberger looked at him, startled, and came to a halt, using the opportunity to free his arm. "What kind of prospects?"

"I'm to write a novel for one of the popular papers. They've already given me the title."

"What?"

"Shh—I don't want the others to find out. They would look down on it—or at least pretend to. But we'll see what Herr Staufner will do when he's forty-five and hasn't a Kreuzer to his name."

"You're writing a novel—" Saxberger couldn't conceal from himself that he was quite impressed. After all, a novel was a substantial piece of work and he respected that. Here, at least among these people, it was something that caught his eye. They assuredly had a tremendous amount of talent between them; work, however, was something they actually did very little of.

"Yes, yes," said Linsmann, "it'll start to come out in six weeks, it's almost completely arranged. Can you lend me five Gulden?"

"Yes," said Saxberger, to his own surprise, because he lent money only in the most exceptional of circumstances. He opened his wallet and handed him the desired banknote. Linsmann put it in his waistcoat pocket without thanking him. He just nodded his head, took Saxberger's arm again and as they—the last of the group—approached the restaurant, he said: "Yes, this is where you end up! Writing pulp novels instead of…"

"Instead of?…"

Linsmann was silent for a while, then, with a short laugh, said, "Instead of doing nothing at all."

As Eduard Saxberger was sitting at home on the following afternoon, his housekeeper came and told him that a woman had arrived. A moment later, Fräulein Gasteiner entered the room. She walked in quite unselfconsciously and with a cheerful smile, as if she'd been expected, and gave her hand to the old gentleman, who hardly had time to recover from his astonishment. She was wearing a little hat and a yellow spring jacket and had her dark boa slung round her neck. In her left hand she was holding a red umbrella and a book.

"I hope I'm not disturbing you," she said, while Saxberger offered her a chair, "but I had to speak to you today, because of the *Wanderings*."

"Oh, of course," said Saxberger, who had stayed standing in front of her.

Fräulein Gasteiner threw back her veil and cast animated glances around the room. "Truly, this is a poet's study," she said. She stood up and went to the window, to where Saxberger followed her. She looked out silently for a while. It was a lovely sunny March day and the nearby hills of the Wienerwald were drawn sharply against the sky. "Wonderful," cried Fräulein Gasteiner, then she turned around and gave the old gentleman her hand for a second time, as if she had to greet him anew.

"My friend," she said, with a slight tremble in her voice. She looked away and then out of the window again. Saxberger remembered how a few days earlier he had yearned for this woman to kiss his hand. He no longer felt that, not since she had been there in his room. There was something about her today that he didn't like. And as he looked at her from the side, he knew what: it was the yellow jacket that he found objectionable.

Fräulein Gasteiner abruptly left the window with a nervous movement of her head, as if she had to shake something off. She sat down at the table and, while pulling the gloves off her fingers, said to Saxberger: "Don't you want to sit with me?"

He took a seat beside her.

She began in a businesslike tone that was in contrast to her previous warmth: "I've brought the *Wanderings*. I read them last night for the... well, I read them again [while saying this, she leafed through the slim volume], with the intention of marking the poems that I wanted to present. I didn't manage it—every poem got a mark." She said all this very matter-of-factly. "So I've come to you, Herr Saxberger, please make the choice yourself!"

She handed him the book. He felt a special pleasure in holding this worn copy in his hand—apparently the same one that Meier had discovered in the second-hand bookshop.

"Well, Fräulein," he said tentatively, "I don't know whether I'll be able to give you good advice in this." He turned the pages pensively. "And also, we have to make sure to end up with things that fit the title 'Evening Moods'."

She smiled. "But that doesn't matter. And if it makes a difference to you, we can just strike out the title on the programme and put something else in instead."

"Maybe this poem," said Saxberger, who was still turning the pages. Already sitting next to him, she moved even closer and looked at the opened page. And she began to read, first quietly, then louder, and finally at full voice and with full expression. It was as if she hadn't initially meant to perform the poem, but been carried away by the verses themselves.

Saxberger listened with relish. To hear these verses read was a sweet, never yet tasted delight. He hardly noticed that it was Fräulein Gasteiner who was reading—he also hardly knew whether he liked the verses or not, but when

Fräulein Gasteiner had finished and it was suddenly quiet in the room and they were sitting very close to each other, he again saw the yellow jacket that bothered him and was especially irritated by a very tender smile that had appeared on the Fräulein's lips and bore no relation to the poem she had just read. He looked away; she took this for a sign that he was inwardly moved.

And at once she began to read a second poem, very loudly, almost shrilly. He thought this must be a habit from the theatre, where she had to speak in large rooms in front of many people. He stood up and went to the window. He tried to imagine what effect this performance would have had in a bigger room—he pictured a full auditorium with the public listening and the verses that he heard resounding through the deep quiet.

Like that, it sounded ever better and the reader's insistent pathos started to come off. It was indeed very good how each word was given its whole worth and how some verses to which he himself had barely paid any more mind were given new and unexpected life. And at the end of the second poem, he said: "Lovely!"

She did not even turn to him, but carried on reading. She stood up, the book in her hand, and from time to time looked up at the old gentleman, but it was the kind of glance with which one looks at a stranger, at an audience. He liked that very much. And then she leafed further on, turning a few pages at once, and read a few more poems as they happened to catch her eye.

Suddenly, she put the book aside and let herself sink into the armchair. She looked at Saxberger, who was standing in motionless thought at the window, and, her face shifting into an expression of suffering, she asked, "Are you satisfied?"

He did not really know how to respond, but came towards her and gave her both hands. She took them sharply, looked him in the eye, then bent down and kissed his right hand. He wanted to pull away—but she held him so tight that he had to let her do it. She bent so far down that he also felt her eyelashes touch him. Eventually, she disengaged her lips and gave him an earnest look. There was an unpleasantly cool, damp patch on the back of the hand she'd kissed. It would have been better if she hadn't done it after all, he thought, and hardly knew why. He said nothing; if she had not kissed his hand, he would have thanked her for the reading—he knew that. But like this it was impossible.

She switched into a bright and candid tone: "Why did you never reply to my letter?"

"Reply?" he repeated mechanically.

"Well, yes," she said, smiling.

He had to admit to himself: it had never even occurred to him.

"Your letter…" he said. "Your letter, I was very pleased to receive it."

She looked at him with a slightly sulky turn to her mouth, which aged her by ten years.

"Very pleased…" she repeated, making a face like a cross child, "and has he got no more than that to say to me?"

In this instant, Herr Saxberger felt that what he would most like to do was throw her out. It struck him very distinctly that only while she was reading his poems had she been at all tolerable.

She saw by a slight twitching of his lips that he was getting anxious, but took it for another sign that he was moved within… She stood up and, as if she had just earned the right to do so, started to go around the room and view the individual pieces of furniture. She did this in an unconstrained, childish manner. She stopped in front of his cupboard and ran her finger across it as if wanting to check for dust. She considered the small smoking table and took the ashtray in her hand to look at it more closely.

She stopped in front of the desk and stroked her fingers across the dark-green folder that lay on it. And all the while—this was what irritated Saxberger the most—she was still wearing that abominable yellow jacket.

While she stood in front of his desk, she said under her breath, as if talking to herself: "So this is where he muses and writes…"

Saxberger feared he would lose his composure, but replied with passable self-control: "No, Fräulein, I don't muse here and I don't write here. I haven't mused and written for thirty years!"

She lifted her gaze and looked with big, sad eyes at the old gentleman—who forced himself to smile, to mitigate the obstinate tone of what he had said—and then spoke with the serene and irrefutable tone of a prophetess:

"You will write again!"

"No!" he almost shouted.

She started at his words, then looked at him timidly.

"No," he repeated more mildly. "I will—unfortunately—not write any more. I can't write any more."

"You don't know that," she replied, "because you don't know the effect that the applause of hundreds of enthusiastic listeners, that the praise of the press—that fame will have on you."

She said this without any exaggeration of tone—with warm and quiet certainty. "Fame"—he made a dismissive gesture and said no more.

"Yes, fame," she said again. He shook his head, but felt strangely reconciled to her.

Just then there was a ringing at the door to his apartment.

"Were you expecting a visitor?" asked Fräulein Gasteiner.

"Not that I know of," replied Saxberger.

The housekeeper came in and reported that Herr Grossinger wished to speak with him.

Fräulein Gasteiner had meanwhile begun to put on her gloves.

"I won't disturb you any longer," she said. "And as for the poems, I think you're happy with the ones I read today."

"Yes, absolutely," responded Herr Saxberger, who had become a little shy, and accompanied her to the door. To Grossinger, who was just walking in, he said, "Please excuse me for just one moment," and he saw the Fräulein as far as the door of his apartment. She pressed his hand almost violently in goodbye. He returned to his room and greeted Grossinger.

"Well, blow me down!" said the delicatessen owner. "Here was I thinking you were dead or at least seriously laid up because you haven't shown your face in the restaurant for more than a week—and all the time… you've been… doing so well!" He glanced meaningfully at the door.

"I'm always well," answered Saxberger in a slightly exasperated voice. "It was very kind of you to make the effort to come up…"

"Actually," interrupted Grossinger, "I'm a deputation— I was supposed to tell you to get better soon from all of us. But I can see that you couldn't really get any better!!" Saxberger decided to pre-empt any more drollery.

"The lady you just met is an actress," he said hastily. "Yes indeed," he added in response to a mischievous smile from Grossinger. "And if you must know why she was here with me, then… then… well, then a week tomorrow go to the recital put on by the 'Enthusiasm' society, where that actress will be reading from my"—he hesitated, and then said firmly: "from my oeuvre."

"What?" asked Grossinger in astonishment—"are you having a laugh?"

"It's quite serious," said Saxberger. "I don't usually speak about it, but I had to discuss some things with the Fräulein, that's why she was here."

"Your oeuvre??" cried Grossinger. "Go on with you! Give over! A public reading? But what's she reading?"

"Poems," said Saxberger… "Here," he added, picking up from his desk a copy of the *Wanderings* that now always lay there.

Grossinger took the book in his hand. "No joke!" he said, "these are rhymes!" And as he looked up laughingly at Saxberger: "That makes us colleagues!" Saxberger knew that Grossinger was thinking of his recent rhyming toast, and answered with dignity: "Almost!"

"And that actress is reading it out?" said Grossinger, shaking his head in wonder. "Hey, Saxberger, we've all got to come. Yes, of course! It'll be a hoot!"

Saxberger clenched his teeth: "You will not come," he said vigorously, "and you will please be so good as not to say anything about it to the others. Oh—not on my account. But there's a whole crowd of gifted youngsters who are putting on the recital, it'll be an artistic, serious audience that comes to the performance—it's a culturally significant event—[he was getting angry because Grossinger was laughing wholeheartedly at what he was hearing]—and there'll be no space for people who don't understand anything about it."

"Don't get yourself worked up! It's already settled! I won't come! Wouldn't dream of it!! I'll be happy not to have to sit through all that palaver! And especially if they're getting old bags like that one to do their declaiming." Again he glanced at the door.

Saxberger said nothing. He disdained this person. Admittedly, this was one of those among whom he had previously lived and whose "conversation" he had shared. And yes, this was one of the least educated among them. But they were all cut from the same cloth. Old philistines! How young he—the "venerable poet"—was when set beside them… He understood that among these people he had *had* to go into a decline. And with that, his anger dissipated. He felt excused before himself. The Grossingers had made the atmosphere around him thick and dull. In it, his free poetic soul could not but suffocate. As he stood there for a full half-minute not saying anything, the good Grossinger began to feel sorry for his mocking words and tried to soften them.

"Well, no harm meant," he said. "She," and he again indicated the door, "she's not bad at all!… An actress, you said? What theatre's she performing at?"

"I don't know," said Saxberger uninterestedly, "where she last was." And feeling that he was allowed to, he added: "I think in Berlin."

"Smashing, smashing," said Grossinger. "Right, then," he continued after a brief pause, "a friendly suggestion! Why don't you come with me to the coffee house?"

"Now?!" said Saxberger.

"Of course! It's almost six. The major must already be waiting for me. And Steininger and Hildebrand'll be there, too. So, are you coming? Seriously, Saxberger, we really were worried about you."

Saxberger decided to go with Grossinger to the coffee house—though not to allay their fears, but because he felt a strange longing rise up in him when Grossinger said these names: a longing to watch and to comment on a game of billiards, and even to keep score. He didn't quite understand it himself, but today he felt more like seeing a game of billiards with these dull philistines than listening to the conversation of his enthusiastic young friends.

"Let's go," he said to Grossinger. "I'll come along."

"Well said!" cried Grossinger, and bit the end off his Cuban cigar.

The recital came closer. And the mood was exalted despite the many adversities that the "Enthusiasm" society had to overcome. Mainly that the newspapers were not taking enough notice of the imminent performance. Each had had the programme sent to it, but they contented themselves merely with writing: "There will be an evening of readings by the 'Enthusiasm' society on such and such an evening in the rooms of the Silver Cross." Only one newspaper, whose editor Blink knew well, printed the programme in full. Ticket sales, which Staufner and Meier took care of, were initially very sluggish. Some of the young people's relatives had ordered tickets and little Winder, who had made great efforts in his family circles, bought ten tickets for which he paid cash up front.

The evenings in the coffee house passed in passionate discussion. Partial rehearsals were held in the restaurant. Bolling read poems by Meier and Fräulein Gasteiner presented a monologue from Christian's "Zenobia".

She was loudly acclaimed. Saxberger was always among them. He was treated with great friendliness and high esteem. Albeit that he couldn't help noticing the deferential tone they had taken at first was no longer present. But he explained that to himself. He had reached such friendly terms with the young people that their deference, which did after all imply a certain unfamiliarity, had necessarily fallen away. He felt very content among them. Fräulein Gasteiner did not come regularly. But when she was there, she almost always sat at his side and looked at him with a gaze in which something faithful and heartfelt was supposed to be communicated. Sometimes she addressed him as "maestro" and once, when they were walking along the street beside each other, she called him "My dear, dear maestro!"

On the day before the recital, when they all stayed long together, she spoke for the first time about her visit to him. "How is my dear little writing room?" she asked. "Is it still as cosy as once it was?" Saxberger found this "as once it was" incongruous, as it had only been a few days, but was otherwise pleased by the question. He treated the actress respectfully, but with deep reserve. Overall, he vacillated in his feelings towards her. Sometimes he thought her very congenial. But he also found that at times he suddenly experienced a violent aversion against her—particularly when she fixed him with her "faithful" gaze.

On this last evening, he was asked by Meier whether he had made an effort "among his friends". At first, he didn't really understand. Then he realized that he, too, had been meant to contribute some ticket sales. "I don't have any friends," he said. "But," objected Meier, "in your circles you must have a lot of admirers?"

"My circle," he said—"as if they were interested in— poetry!" And he told the young man about his conversation with Grossinger.

Meier smiled. "You shouldn't have been so dismissive. What goes through their heads is all the same to us. Once they're sitting in there, they're the public and the public's what we need... the more, the better."

The evening again ended late and very jovially, with a toast of Staufner's to "our" Saxberger.

He spent the next day in a quiet, agreeable mood. He was looking forward to the recital, to the reading of his poems, to the applause. About the others he thought very little. How much did they still have ahead of them! A whole life. But he, too, might still have a few things ahead of him. If Fräulein Gasteiner had indeed been right and if fame... no, no, he didn't want to expect too much.

In the late afternoon, Saxberger left his apartment. It was so warm that he wore his surtout open over his black frock coat.

He reached the Silver Cross half an hour before the recital was due to begin. He had to walk through a hallway, the courtyard and then a short corridor, where the cloakroom was, to reach the doors to the function room. Meier and Winder were already standing there. Beside them was one of the Cross's serving staff, in slightly too long, machine-made white gloves, who was to collect the tickets. The corridor still seemed to hold all the odours of the recent carnival. (Small dances were also frequently held there.) It smelt of beer, tobacco, faded perfume, of damp clothes, mouldy wood and gas.

Meier led the old gentleman through the function room, which was still hardly lit: only three, four low gas flames were burning in their brackets on the walls. The tables were laid. In the background, on the platform, stood a smaller table with two candles on it. Meier accompanied Saxberger into a little back room. The friends were gathered there, all in black frock coats of a more modern cut.

Saxberger was greeted with a "hurrah" that sounded a touch muted. Meier immediately took off again. Friedinger and Blink were sitting at a committee table in the middle of the room and drinking beer. Linsmann, the manuscript of his speech in his hand, was pacing up and down, and kept knocking into the stand on which they'd hung their hats and coats. As Saxberger came in, Blink was discoursing to Staufner, who was sitting on the table and swinging his legs. Christian and the actor Bolling were standing in a corner, where they were embroiled in an emphatic debate to which they returned right after the "hurrah". Saxberger went over to them with the words, "Well, kids, what's got into you?"

"This person," replied Bolling, pointing at Christian, "is quite simply an idiot."

"You don't want to—that's all there is to it," said Christian.

"I can't give a monologue without preparation—and a female one at that, it won't work! I'll embarrass us both."

"Oh," asked Saxberger, "what monologue is that?"

"The one from 'Zenobia'," said Bolling… "because that wench…" he corrected himself, "because Fräulein Gasteiner doesn't feel like it."

"What?" exclaimed Saxberger in concern. "What's happened to Fräulein Gasteiner?"

"She's ill," said Christian. "She might not come."

Saxberger was intensely shocked. "And this is something you tell me just like that? Who's going to read my poems?"

"Right!" said Bolling. "That number would have to be dropped as well."

"But what's wrong with Fräulein Gasteiner, when did she fall ill?" cried Saxberger.

"It's not dangerous," responded Christian, "a migraine, which might still get better."

"Might!" repeated Saxberger, almost in tears.

"Oh, come on," said Bolling, "they've had another spat and she wants to wind him up, that's all it is! Migraine! Haha—Gasteiner's migraine—haha!"

"But it's totally inconsiderate," cried Saxberger. He was no longer thinking of anything but his own part of the programme. He was wholly indifferent to everything else.

Blink, without coming any closer to them, joined in the conversation. "Don't worry, Herr Saxberger—Gasteiner will come, you can be sure of that."

"But if she doesn't come," cried Saxberger, "who's going to read my poems?"

No one spoke. They were all wholly indifferent to Saxberger's poems.

In that instant, Saxberger hated the whole company. The way he saw it, they should have greeted his arrival in sheer despair, should have clustered around him: "Do you already know, Gasteiner can't come, we'll have to cancel the recital, we'll have to postpone it." None of that. They couldn't have been cooler, not even—no, not even if it was just that Friedinger hadn't come to read his comic novelette.

Then Blink said coldly: "Here she is." And already they could see floating out of the half-dark of the function room a white female figure, who approached the door and finally, Meier at her side, walked in smiling. It was Ludwiga Gasteiner in a white, deeply décolleté evening dress. Round her shoulders hung a slightly shabby raincoat. In her hand she carried a pair of very long light-yellow gloves.

"Can it be that I'm the last one here?" she said harmlessly, while waving a bright greeting to all sides. And, letting herself sink at once into an armchair, she sighed deeply and said: "Oh, kids, I really thought I was going to have to cancel on you! My skull was about to burst. I've had six antipyrine sachets."

Meier left again and closed the door behind him. In the function room, they were beginning to turn up the gas lamps. The first guests had arrived.

Saxberger was now vexed with himself for having expressed his fears so undisguisedly. Especially as he could feel Blink giving him an ironic look.

Friedinger half opened the door, glanced into the function room and turned back to the others. "People!!" he said.

"I'm just curious," opined Staufner, "about how the papers will cover it. Whether the *Neue Freie*, for example, will send someone."

"Surely not," said Fräulein Gasteiner, "even if only because my name's in the programme. If they could, they'd have destroyed me long ago."

"In any case, the papers aren't the main thing," said Blink. "It's about the audience." Through the half-opened door came a noise of chairs being shifted. Staufner had a look. "It's filling up," he said. "But it's still crazy of you," said Bolling, "to have had tables laid out. It'll spoil the atmosphere if they're all eating."

"On the contrary," retorted Staufner. "And they've been given strict instructions not to serve anything during the performance."

"So," Fräulein Gasteiner turned to Saxberger, "are you already very excited?"

He was annoyed by the question.

"Don't worry," said Blink, taking the old gentleman encouragingly by the arm, "there's not much that can happen!"

He really was being treated like someone making his debut, someone whose spirits had to be buoyed up, who needed to have allowances made... He did not reply. Fräulein Gasteiner put the book on the table in front of her and appeared to be reading over the poems. From time to time she looked up at Saxberger with a smile. Linsmann began to declaim loudly:

"Ladies and gentlemen... For years, a battle has been raging in the blossoming meadows of German art. For years..." he mumbled again.

Bolling was standing in front of a mirror and practising his facial expressions.

Outside, it was getting ever louder. They heard the

voices of the arriving guests. The noise of tables and chairs being shifted became more distinct. Saxberger cast a glance into the function room and, for the first time, he felt his heart beat a little faster. Yes, truly, here they came. These were the people who would sit and listen for an uninterrupted quarter of an hour to his verses. These were the people who would clap their hands and be dumbfounded that the poet of these verses had remained unknown for decades.

Meier came in. "We can start in five minutes... it's almost quarter past seven."

"Is there anyone there from the papers?" asked Staufner.

Meier shook his head. "But maybe I don't know one or another of them."

"Linsmann," said Staufner, "get ready."

"Already am," he replied.

Fräulein Gasteiner flashed Saxberger a smile and whispered, "Time to face the music!"

"Linsmann, you're on," said Staufner.

Linsmann rasped his throat, stepped out into the function room and paused briefly in the doorway without being noticed by the audience. Then, after a deep breath, he climbed the few steps to the podium, set the manuscript in front of him and sat down. Some people shouted "Bravo!", there was a commotion in the room. The gentlemen in the back room stayed near the half-open door in order not to miss a single word of the lecture, nor any of the impression that it would surely make on the audience.

Little Winder stood at the entrance and raised his eyebrows to greet a group of very young people—classmates from his school, to whom he had propagandized on behalf of "Enthusiasm". And Linsmann began: "Ladies, gentlemen! For years, a battle of minds has been raging in the blossoming meadows of German art…"

The room was almost completely still. A few more young people arrived during the lecture and, so as not to cause any disruption, stayed by the doors. Linsmann spoke with a sonorous voice and in some moments the magniloquent phrases about the banner of an ideal, about true and chaste art, about honest and humble striving, sounded so fresh and so pure that it was as if they were emerging out of deep conviction from the speaker's breast.

The lecture was followed by noisy applause and the atmosphere in the room was good. Linsmann even had to come out again and give a bow. Blink was almost unpleasantly astonished by the efficacy of his speech. He was annoyed that he hadn't delivered it himself—after all, he had written virtually the whole thing. He shook

Linsmann's hand half ironically and Linsmann thanked him with feeling.

Saxberger had found it boring. Over the past week, he had heard all these phrases till he was sick of them and Linsmann's pathos no longer had any effect on him. He was leaning against the door with Fräulein Gasteiner standing behind him and sometimes he could feel the touch of her breath on his hair.

After a short interlude, Staufner stepped out. He looked around the audience before beginning and then recited a ballad. It was the first thing of his that Saxberger had heard. Beside him, Friedinger said to Blink: "Would it really be too much for him to have written something new in the last three years?"

Staufner became very vehement in the course of his declamation; he shouted so excessively that eventually his voice cracked. Saxberger involuntarily turned to look at Fräulein Gasteiner, who was laughing heartily. Bolling— as a joke, of course—held his hands over his ears, and a quiet giggling could be heard from the audience. Staufner got himself back under control and everything went well from then on. After the ballad there was some not very loud applause. Staufner then read two short poems that went down better. But he didn't seem quite satisfied as he, after being called back twice by the audience, returned to his friends.

Now it was supposed to be the turn of the "Evening Moods", as it was still called in the programme. His young friends were not behaving as Saxberger had expected. They chatted to one another without paying him any attention, as if this business had nothing to do with them. Only Fräulein Gasteiner gripped him by the hand: "Time for this evening to prove itself," she whispered to him. It suddenly struck him how much depended on the next few minutes. He imagined an intoxicating, deafening success that would reach the world outside. He thought of how the audience would be moved and amazed when he showed them his face… and he also imagined resounding laughter that would spring up during the recital and annihilate him.

"Break a leg!" was whispered from beside him. It was the voice of Fräulein Gasteiner, who had taken Meier's arm and was going on. He quickly pressed her hand, he felt very well disposed towards her.

As she stepped up to the podium, clapping rang out more loudly than any they had heard so far. Saxberger was pleased. Behind him, Staufner, Blink and Friedinger were talking. He turned around and called out "Shh." Before he turned back, he saw the smiles with which they looked at one another. From then on, he kept his eyes firmly on Fräulein Gasteiner.

"Evening Moods," she said. She read in a rocking, sensual tone that was completely unfamiliar to him. The audience was deeply quiet and, as he looked at the people, he could see that all their gazes were fixed upon the reader. When the poem came to an end—there was silence. Saxberger could not understand it, then he thought, perhaps they didn't know that it was over. But the applause was already breaking out. The second between the last word and the beginning of the ovation had felt very long to him.

Fräulein Gasteiner gently inclined her head in thanks and carried on reading. She read another three poems, all of which were heartily received. It was just that, to Saxberger, she didn't seem to be giving the audience enough time to cheer themselves out—and so denied him a last little bit of applause each time she started on a new poem. But when she had finished and Meier accompanied her off, and the ovation continued, she took Saxberger by the hand to pull him up onto the podium. He really did not want to go. She went back up alone and one of the serving staff presented her with a small laurel wreath, and when she went off with it and the applause rang out again—she again took the poet by the hand and this time he had to let himself be led out onto the podium… yes, the moment had come. The ovation roared around him. He felt nothing in particular, hardly even the embarrassment he had feared. He had to go up again—this time without Fräulein Gasteiner, and it was a little peculiar to him to hear the noise of clapping hands and the loud shouts of "Bravo". He bowed several times, turned to the door and then, just as the clapping was getting weaker, he heard a voice from slightly behind him, or to the side—he couldn't quite tell—but the words were perfectly distinct, no matter how quietly they had been said: "Poor devil!" He wanted to look around, but he felt that that would seem absurd. The applause ended… he heard the audience going back to murmuring. He stayed, as if there were no other place for him, standing at the door where he had stood before. And still those words echoed within him… "poor devil!"—what was that supposed to mean? Why? Why? And while his young friends surrounded him, shook his hand, congratulated him and Fräulein Gasteiner hung the laurel wreath round his neck, he thought to himself: why "poor devil"? What was it about? Because I'm old? Do I really look that wretched? Or is it just that I behaved ridiculously when I was bowing? And as he heard the words "poor devil" sounding again and again in his ears, they took on an ever

sadder, more pitying tone… tears ran down his face, but
he knew: it was not from the emotion of his success—no,
it was unbearable hurt, his anger at the incomprehensible
words of a stranger he would never find.

But the young people around him believed themselves to
understand very well why the old gentleman was crying. And
Friedinger said to Blink: "Well, you can hardly begrudge
him that!"

And still Saxberger stood wordlessly by the door, while
Bolling appeared on the podium to read some poems by
Geibel, Lenau and Goethe. He looked up and caught sight
of himself in the mirror that hung opposite the door. His
own expression seemed alien, almost uncanny to him—it
was odd how crying had altered his features. And there,
round his neck—oh yes, it was still there, the wreath that
Gasteiner had hung on him. He took it off and put it on
a chair.

The others stayed by the door to listen to Bolling. He sat
down at the table; Fräulein Gasteiner took a seat opposite
him.

"Well, were you satisfied?" she whispered tenderly to him.

He just nodded. Then it occurred to him that he had
to thank her. He reached his hand to her across the table
and said, "Thank you."

"But why are you so sad?" she asked.

"Me?—oh no!—" he said. It was incredible how much this hurt him. It was as if someone had let him see a great sorrow that was weighing on him and that until then he had known nothing about…

He stayed sitting where he was; he felt entirely drained and exhausted.

After Bolling had finished, to great applause, Gasteiner went up again and presented the monologue from "Zenobia". The door to the larger room was half open and Saxberger could hear every word. It was from the first act, which Saxberger had read. He thought the monologue was hollow and boring and, as she finished it, thunderous applause again broke out. She was called back twice.

When he thought about it, the audience always applauded. And he was no longer sure whether the clapping after his poems had been significantly louder than after the other readings. And it was, after all, unlikely that they were saying "poor devil" about Christian as he took his bow. They might have said "talentless fraud" or "boring sort of a man"—but… "poor devil"… no, not that.

He stood up and congratulated Christian, who had come across to the table with Fräulein Gasteiner. She said quietly to the young man: "The ovation wasn't on my account!" Christian kissed her on the arm. During the next number, Saxberger stood at the door and watched the audience with the vague desire, despite everything, to find the person from whose lips those words might have come. It was impossible.

At one of the nearest tables Saxberger recognized some people he had sometimes seen in the coffee house where "Enthusiasm" met. Some young girls were also there who, when his head again appeared at the door, elbowed and hissed at one another that there was Saxberger. But in general, the audience was already focused and listening to Bolling read Meier's poems. Saxberger was familiar with them. They came from the book that the young man had once given him. They were passable verses. He wondered whether they were just as good—as his own? Whether they were ultimately better? Everything had again become so unclear. He asked himself whether it took any especial art to put together a few passable verses as a young man and whether he himself had achieved anything more than that… but hadn't they discovered and venerated him— there had to be a reason for it!

Bolling had finished. And again the applause broke out. It really was too stupid. Each and every time these calls of bravo and this clapping-together of hands—let it always mean the same! Everyone was applauded—but only he was a poor devil!! Why? Why? Perhaps it was to do with his coat?… No, no, it was completely flawless, elegant almost. Shabby was something he never looked. It must be because he had only now—as an old man—received the recognition he deserved. There had been nothing malicious in those words, nothing in the least. But then why did they make him so dreadfully unhappy?

Two good eyes were gazing at him from across the room. It was little Winder, who was standing faithful and conscientious at the door, and who, as he saw that his respectful gaze had been noticed, quickly looked away. The last up was Friedinger, who threw himself into an amusing novelette about student life. The applause for him was the most appreciative of all. The audience had already thinned out somewhat, but those still present laughed uproariously, and at the end he was called back with a storm of cheers.

When it was all over, some of the society members' acquaintances and relatives came into the small back room to say the usual kind or exuberant things to the group of friends. Some men Saxberger didn't know came over and congratulated him. By and by, everyone left, with the exception of a few still sitting at their tables to drink a last glass of beer.

Little Winder came in and, blushing, said to Saxberger: "It was really very good."

The friends sat down together, drank quite a lot and were in high spirits. But Saxberger slipped away. He sat alone in a cab and was driven home. As he leant into the corner with his eyes closed, he thought about how the evening to which he had looked forward so much was already over. And what now?... Oh, this certainly wasn't fame. Some people perhaps even still mention him today and say: those were lovely poems, those by Saxberger... and others: yes, if only he had been discovered at the right time. And some say: poor devil...

Where might he be, the one who said that?

The cab shook him about on the uneven surface, rattling the badly mounted windows. And Saxberger was unhappier than he had long been.

*   *   *

On the following morning, Saxberger woke up dully disgruntled. The mechanical activity of his morning in the office did him good, since it did not give him a chance to really reflect. On the way home from his midday meal, he was surprised by how warm it was. Little girls were selling bunches of violets in the streets, those out for a stroll were already walking at the leisurely pace with which one saunters on the first beautiful, mild day. Spring had come.

Saxberger, having got back to his apartment, opened the window. The air that came from outside did him good. He propped his elbows on the windowsill and looked out. He began to feel sleepy, his eyes were falling shut and, when he thought of the previous evening, it seemed very far away.

But he felt a restlessness. Soon it propelled him towards the coffee house and on the walk there he was overcome by keen curiosity about what might be in the papers. He found the company in an excited mood and was greeted as a close companion, without much deference.

In the morning papers there had been nothing and there was nothing yet in the evening papers published so far. Staufner was particularly annoyed.

"If it was just us, fine—then I wouldn't say anything," he told them. "We're young people—it's just the way of things for them to put obstacles in our path, but I mean we do have one person among us who…" and he looked up at Saxberger, who felt very uncomfortable. He would much rather not have been there.

Just then, the waiter put a new evening paper on the table and Staufner interrupted himself at once: "Perhaps there's something in here." He picked it up. Blink immediately discovered a review. "There's something here," he said.

And Saxberger felt his heart beating in his chest.

"Ah!!" cried Staufner, his face darkening.

"Well... what is it... read it! Read it... Listen!..."

He read: "A literary society with the promising name of 'Enthusiasm' staged a recital yesterday. Several young gentlemen—though it must be said that some of these young gentlemen were already somewhat long in the tooth—felt a pressing desire to read their more or less realized productions to a number of well-disposed friends, or to have them read by several artistic colossi unknown to a wider audience. There can be no objection to this and we have no desire to disturb these young gentlemen at their harmless pastime. It just seemed superfluous to have their various trifles prefaced by a sort of keynote address, in which the young gentlemen were pleased to present themselves as the rightful heralds of the one true redemptive form of Art. Well, we have to say: the young gentlemen know how to blow a trumpet, but not much else!"

"Idiot," added Staufner so quickly that it was as if he were reading the reviewer's byline.

There was a brief silence. The page was ripped out of Staufner's hand and passed around.

"Scandalous... that's the state of Viennese criticism... impertinent misrepresentation... journalistic humour... cretin... who can it have been..."

Fräulein Gasteiner had just come in and saw they were all bending over the page at once, some sitting, one looking over the heads of the others. "What have you got there?"

She sat down and read along with them. When she had finished, she said no more than: "You can thank Herr Linsmann for that."

"What?" Linsmann said threateningly.

"Of course"—responded Fräulein Gasteiner. "Your speech!!"

Linsmann leapt to his feet, wanted to retaliate. But he was pushed back down into his seat. He shook his head contemptuously and just mumbled something malicious through gritted teeth.

"Why did you say *you* can thank him for it?" asked Staufner. "You're not wholly uninvolved yourself, are you?!"

"There's no mention of me whatsoever," Fräulein Gasteiner responded coldly.

"Excuse me," screeched Staufner. "It's right here... 'artistic colossi unknown to a wider audience'."

"I can read... but you don't think that refers to me?"

"I suppose just to me," mocked Bolling.

"Probably," said Fräulein Gasteiner. "The fact that it doesn't refer to me is something I can prove to you. [She pulled a piece of paper from the pocket of her dress.] I've just signed."

"For Großjedlersdorf," screamed Staufner, who had completely lost his composure.

"No, for Neuruppin…" Fräulein Gasteiner said calmly.

Staufner emitted a short laugh. Christian cast a fearful and questioning glance at the actress. Saxberger noticed it. And in the same moment, Fräulein Gasteiner, with a sideways look at the old gentleman, said: "Nothing now will keep me from my art…"

"In Neuruppin," said Friedinger, "even Staufner and his ballads could be a hit."

"You're a clot," screamed Staufner. "There's not a word in here about my ballads. I know very well what this idiot's snide little remarks are supposed to mean—I know it precisely!…"

"Keep it down," said Meier… "them over there"—and he gestured at the neighbouring table, "they've definitely seen the piece as well."

Indeed, some of the "talentless ones" had turned briefly towards them.

Saxberger sat without saying anything while the shouts and the talk buzzed around him. He hadn't really grasped it yet… he had seen the paper. It was the same one which a few days earlier had announced that, among others, the venerable poet Saxberger had agreed to take part. And after that friendly—if not admiring—mention, it was aiming these derisive phrases at him out of all of them. It was incomprehensible… He asked himself what he had ever done to those people?… "Several young gentlemen, some of them already somewhat long in the tooth…" Was it even allowed, to take a decent person who had done nothing wrong and treat him like this? Long in the tooth… that was meant scornfully, he felt it—they were making fun of his age—of how he, the old fool, had started to associate himself with this circle of young people among whom he simply did not belong—with this society, by being with whom he declared himself to be just beginning.

And they, why weren't they saying anything to him? Why weren't they explaining that it was possible their meagre attempts didn't yet add up to much and that they still looked respectfully up to him—yes, why weren't they apologizing, as would only have been proper, instead of speaking across each other and talking about themselves and then more about themselves and asserting that they were great geniuses after all and that they would show everyone.

And Staufner even turned to him to say, in an unmistakably sarcastic tone, "Well, and how do you feel about all this, maestro Saxberger?"

"Me?" he asked, but couldn't say any more. He sensed that this "maestro" was not meant sincerely.

"Come on," said Meier, smiling, "there's no need for despair, not even if the idiot happened to be right and we really didn't offer very much. We'll just do it better next time, won't we?" he added, looking at Saxberger as though this remark might also apply to him.

"Gentlemen," said Saxberger, with a slight tremor in his voice, "I've already done it as well as I can… and you did all like it."

"Hold on, hold on," cried the others, "who here's talking about the *Wanderings*? Hurrah for the *Wanderings*, hurrah for Saxberger!"

Saxberger held up his hand in protest. "No, no… I just mean, I'm not one of those who will still do better, I'm a bit too old for that."

He smiled bitterly.

The conversation became quieter and the mood more conciliatory. They eventually agreed that they had got far more worked up than they needed to about this stupid review. This sort of thing happened to everyone when they were starting out. Yes, it would all be different when the books they were working on were published; this kind of nonsense was just what everyone had to put up with.

"Oh, for the love of God, Winder," said Friedinger, and gave the little boy, who was sitting there disconsolately, a clap on the shoulder. "Why such a sad face, don't let it get to you!"

"I… I—I can't help it," said Winder, so seriously and dolefully that the others had to laugh.

The waiter came and brought another evening newspaper. It was one of the less widely distributed papers, which they otherwise never read. Today, however, Staufner picked it up at once.

"There's nothing in there," said Friedinger.

"Oh ho," said Staufner, and lifted his right index finger. They all fell silent and he read:

"A recital by Vienna's best-known…" he looked up… "best-known literary society, 'Enthusiasm', took place yesterday. Poems and novelettes by the young authors were read aloud, in part by established stage figures, and met with thunderous approval from the audience. The young poets, among whom were Messrs Staufner, Meier,

Saxberger and Linsmann, doubtless merit the greatest hopes for the future, even if the fermenting must has not in all cases yet been transformed into powerful wine…"

Staufner put the newspaper down, and at first no one spoke.

"Well, that's all right…" he finally said.

"That's all right?" Bolling asked with heavy sarcasm.

"Of course, after all, it's—at least it means well!"

"You think?" asked Bolling even more sarcastically… "All right then. Good night." He laughed curtly, took his hat and went.

"Thespian vanity," whispered Friedinger to Christian, without noticing that the latter was sitting beside Fräulein Gasteiner and clutching her hand to prevent her from leaving.

Pale with rage, she said: "I find one thing priceless, that on the basis of a speech written by Herr Blink, Herr Linsmann is held to be a promising poet…"

"Who said," retorted Linsmann, "that this man has not read my other work?"

"He has read it," said Meier definitively.

"Why…"

"This review," said Meier, "is thanks to me."

"How… what… don't talk nonsense…"

"It's true. From next month, I'm going to be a theatre reviewer for this paper, and I used my connections."

"It's by you?…" repeated Staufner.

"Indeed."

"Then you're a very vulgar piece of work," shrieked Staufner, and so shifted the ambiguous mood into a sudden clarity. "This," and he banged his hand on the paper, "this is how a friend writes about us? These laughable banalities, that are nothing and mean nothing, are how you dismiss us?"

"Fermenting must, are we?" Friedinger screamed over him.

"I'm a fermenting must," screamed Linsmann.

"Ahahaha," laughed Staufner, and read with ironic emphasis: "…the young poets doubtless merit, hahaha, doubtless merit the greatest hopes… hopes… an idiot is what you are, and presumptuous to boot."

Meier tried in vain to make himself understood. "The review wasn't written by me, I just arranged it so they covered the recital… I just gave them the dates."

"You should have given them other dates," shouted Staufner. "You either stand up for something or you don't…"

At this, Meier too became angry. "I did what I could.

I couldn't accept a new job and then use it right away to do some advertising for my friends."

"Advertising! Haha…"

"Damn it, I can't. You can see, I didn't write a single syllable more about myself."

"Write!! Write!!"

"No, not write—influence. I didn't say one word more for myself than for any of you…"

"Marvellous," cried Staufner, "marvellous! Shall I tell you in one word what you are?—A careerist!"

"Well," cried Meier, "and do you want to hear in two words what you lot are—an ungrateful…" he held back the second word.

"Gratitude is what he wants, you hear that?" shouted Staufner.

It grew so loud at the table that shushing noises came at them from around the coffee house.

"He wants gratitude!" said Staufner in a lowered voice. "It's outrageous, he's lost all self-control."

"You owe me," retorted Meier. "Remember what I've done for you—even aside from that panegyric, for which I came close to compromising myself at the newspaper. Just remember… all that I've got hold of for you…" and in that moment his gaze touched almost imperceptibly on the old gentleman, Saxberger, who was sitting painfully ill at ease, embarrassed and unhappy amid this argument and staying only because he couldn't summon the courage to leave.

"Go back to your paper," screamed Staufner. "We'll get on just fine without you."

Meier stood up, took his hat and went without saying goodbye. He did not even say anything to old Saxberger, and went so far as to cast a poisonous glance at innocent little Winder.

"It's suffocating in here today," said Fräulein Gasteiner, who had gone first pale, now red with anger, and, as she stood up—she was again wearing the yellow jacket—she added: "I'm leaving. Are you coming, Christian?" She threw it at him like an order. Christian rose as well, said "Excuse me" and accompanied Fräulein Gasteiner out. At the door, she turned around a last time and waved conspicuously. Saxberger could not but notice that the parting was for him. He inclined his head.

"The old ham's going to ruin that stupid boy."

"Old ham…" Saxberger had to nod to himself in agreement. He realized all at once that he had known that for a long time.

"It really is getting unbearable in here," said Staufner. Let's go outside… shall we?"

They stood. The waiter brought their coats and hats. They went out onto the street.

"Good night, gentlemen," said Saxberger.

"You're not coming with us?" asked Staufner.

"Thank you, but I'm tired."

"Till tomorrow then," said Staufner. They shook his hand, all quite cool and thoughtless—he was alone.

The evening was beautiful and, after the oppressive atmosphere of the coffee house, it was a solace to Saxberger to have the soft, quiet air move around him. The scene he had just witnessed had initially been almost incomprehensible to him. That these people were so furious just because Meier hadn't praised them more than he had!… If he himself were to make any criticism of the review… he had been just slightly annoyed while it was being read by the cursoriness with which the report, in mentioning promising young poets, had named him as one of them. But when he heard that Meier had composed the review—then, then he had been astounded by the indifference of that gentleman, who only a few weeks previously had enthusiastically conveyed to him the tributes of Young Vienna… The enthusiasm had blown over a bit too rapidly—it must have occurred to them quite soon that they had come thirty or forty years too late. They hardly even took him seriously any more. What a change there had been in the way these young people spoke to him.

He realized that someone was walking alongside him. It was little Winder, who had already been there for some time without the old gentleman noticing. "What, you're accompanying me? I'm sorry, I didn't even see you."

"Oh, please, please…" said little Winder. "I didn't want to disturb you—I just—"

"Would you like something from me?" asked the old gentleman in a very friendly voice.

"Yes… a great, great favour—I've wanted to ask it for ever, because I have such great, such heartfelt respect for you—"

Saxberger looked at him benevolently. For all that he tangled himself up, the young man was telling the truth. His self-conscious words sounded genuine.

"Well, what is it that you would like to ask me for?"

"I kept not daring to ask—you're always so sought after—and then, how many things have people already turned to you for… you see, it's about me personally"—he added nervously.

"Well?" asked Saxberger.

"It's that I would very much like to—I would like a candid judgement, an honest one from your own mouth, on whether I have talent or not… yes, you I can trust, it's you I'd like to leave the decision to, because you should know, Herr Saxberger, my parents are very much against it."

"And how am I supposed to decide whether you have talent?"

"That's just it. I'd like to give you my stuff to read—I'd like—"

Saxberger raised a hand to ward him off. "My dear Herr Winder, please don't take it badly, but it would be better if you didn't… Of course you can give me your things to read, but a judgement—no, no—"

Little Winder became very sad. "But why?" he asked.

"Well," replied Saxberger, and it came as a great relief to suddenly find the right words: "I don't understand the first thing about it!"

"You, Herr Saxberger??"

"I give you my word, I don't understand the first thing. If something was very beautiful or very bad, I might be able to tell you the difference, but to say whether you have talent or not?"

"But who can tell me then, if not you?"

"It's difficult, without question—and especially difficult for people as young as you. While someone's young, they might manage to get a few things together… and then… then it's just over and you don't know how it ended."

"But I understand that very well," said Winder, "that after a while you lose your pleasure in it, if you aren't getting any encouragement or any recognition."

"You think so?…" asked Saxberger, and thought for a few seconds. "And who, in the end, can guarantee you the encouragement and recognition?"

"Well, if you yourself felt like reading my pieces, you, Herr Saxberger, and then encouraged me…"

"Me, Herr Saxberger! Who am I, this Herr Saxberger? Who do you think I am?"

"Oh…"

"Maybe the young Saxberger was something—it's possible, I don't know it myself any more, because I no longer understand anything at all about it." He was quiet. "My dear Herr Winder," he then said, "go to someone else—I don't really know why you've settled on me in the first place. The *Wanderings*! Tell me honestly—did you even like them that much? What was it that you liked about them?"

"The *Wanderings*?—Well… it's the *Wanderings* that I haven't read yet."

The old gentleman stopped dead, truly startled. But then, as he saw this young person standing in front of him and staring shamefacedly at the ground, he had to laugh.

"You've not read them? Well, why, well—then why on earth do you admire me so much?"

Little Winder looked up at him again. "I just have such a boundless trust in you—you're completely different from the others. Much friendlier in how you treat me. The others don't take any notice of me. Please, Herr Saxberger, Meier promised that he would lend me the *Wanderings*—he promised all of us—but it just shows you can't rely on other people."

"All of you?... So none of you have actually—"

Saxberger laughed. He laughed as heartily as he long hadn't. "Let's make a deal," he said to Winder, giving him his hand. "You don't need to read my poems and in exchange I won't read yours either—all right?"

"Herr Saxberger, are you angry with me?"

"But, child! The thought hadn't crossed my mind."

They had reached the old gentleman's usual restaurant and Saxberger instinctively came to a halt. "I've reached where I'm going," he said. "Thank you for keeping me company—and if you ever want to visit me, it would be a pleasure."

"... Herr Saxberger—"

"Goodbye, Herr Winder, get home safely!" With those words, the old gentleman left little Winder standing where he was and opened the door to the restaurant where his old group of friends habitually met.

The air that billowed out smelt of beer, smoke and food. The well-known voices were talking over one another, loud and laughing. And it seemed to him that he was returning from a short, troublesome journey to a home that he had never loved but in which he now rediscovered the soft and muffled comforts of before. He sensed that he no longer wanted anything more, no longer needed anything more. He remained standing in the doorway for just a second, then strode decisively to his table, breathed out deeply and sat down with a smile. He knew no one would ever say "poor devil" about him here.

Little Winder stayed outside for a few minutes after the door had closed. Tears were in his eyes. He shook his head: I was wrong about him, he said to himself, and felt very abandoned as he slowly wended his way back through the quiet streets to the coffee house.

AFTERWORD

A longing for late fame awakes in Eduard Saxberger at an advanced age, when the *Wanderings*, the lyrical work of the early years in which he wrote poetry, is discovered by the young literary circle "Enthusiasm". Memories of the time when he himself was "one of the best and proudest in a circle of young people who [...] did not want to be anything but artists" make him aware of the tragedy of his "whole sorry life". Elevated by his new devotees, by "Young Vienna", to the status of idol and "maestro", Saxberger readily adopts their idea of him as his own self-image: "I am a poet." His life as a civil servant he now considers only a "mask" behind which he has had to hide for all these years.

As, however, he is quickly forced to realize that he has come a very long way from his days as a poet and become completely estranged from his early work, the story experiences its first crisis and turning point, an instance of peripeteia as described in Gustav Freytag's theory of drama—and Schnitzler's estate also contains a sketch with the title "On the venerable poet as a drama".[1]

Even the scene of Saxberger's former poetic inspiration, where the best verses had always come easily to him, the banks of the Danube canal, is no longer as it was: the "whistling of locomotives and the distant groaning of the steam trams", the "tall factory smokestacks [that] stretched above them into the sky" and the "miserably dressed people" all belong to the backdrop of a modern city. Saxberger does not see himself as equal to the impressions of the modern world's sounds and images—the aesthetic stimuli of a radical modernity—and so "the few poor thoughts he had already caught were fluttering off again". The final crisis, however, and the "catastrophe" in Freytag's sense, befalls the protagonist at an evening of recitals put on by the young literati, when, after some of his own poems have been read, he hears amid the thunderous applause someone in the audience say the words, "Poor devil". Words that resonate constantly in his head and determine all his thoughts thereafter—very similarly to the "stupid boy" said by the baker in Schnitzler's *Lieutenant Gustl*. The story's downward spiral then takes its course inexorably.

*

In this novella, Schnitzler also addresses the, for him sometimes so vexed, question of the negative dialectic between
artistic work and the bourgeois life. "Med[ical] and poet[ic]
worldviews are beating each other up in the most amusing
fashion in my so-c[alled] soul",[2] reads his diary entry on
17th April 1880, and at the beginning of that year he had
already given himself this far from rosy prognosis: "If I were
only as much of an artist as I have an artist's temperament
[...] my future will be: ending up a mediocre doctor!"[3]

The literary society "Enthusiasm's" self-imposed absten-
tion from anything that smells of life, anything embarrass-
ingly redolent of "monotonous employment", is unmasked
in the novella as merely a pose affected by young artists. The
story's comedy derives from the ironic distance between,
on the one hand, the characters, who believe themselves
to be intelligently discussing art, and, on the other, the
nuanced and psychologically detailed voice of the narrator,
who reveals the superficiality and triteness of their ideal
of "true and chaste art" and mercilessly strips away their
clichés and slogans: "Ultimately, all lyrical poems are either
morning moods or evening moods," one of their number
pronounces, "Or night moods". Just as subtly constructed
are the parallels, the structural correspondences between
the petty bourgeois regulars at the "Pickled Pear" and the

young artists' circle: in both there are toasts and laudatory speeches, in both they are "talking and shouting over one another", and with neither does Saxberger truly fit in. The bright yellow raincoat mentioned in a speech by Grossinger, a delicatessen owner whom Saxberger views with scorn, is subject to a transference that all but begs to be interpreted in the terms of psychoanalysis: the light yellow gloves and particularly the "yellow spring jacket" worn by the eccentric actress Fräulein Gasteiner are seen by Saxberger, whom she reveres with libidinous undertones, as intensely unpleasant.

To what extent should Schnitzler's portrait of literary bohemianism, the "Young Vienna" of the novella, be understood as a parody of the literary circle that met in the Café Griensteidl in the centre of the city?[4] "Young Austria. In the Griensteidl,"[5] noted Schnitzler in his diary on 26th February 1891. Alongside the inner circle—Hugo von Hofmannsthal, Richard Beer-Hofmann, Felix Salten, Hermann Bahr and Schnitzler—many other, mostly long-forgotten writers, journalists and artists gathered in an open, fluctuating and heterogeneous group—"12 people in the c-h,"[6] noted Schnitzler on, for example, 3rd December 1892.

The Young Viennese and the "Enthusiasts" are bound together by their idea of themselves as staying "apart from those following the beaten track", the literary mainstream, by keeping their distance from the "careerists" who simply follow what is fashionable, and also by the concomitant conundrum: "The newspapers take no notice of us. [...] Who's ever heard of our 'Enthusiasm' society?" And the solution is: "We have to put on readings." The Young Viennese, too, feared they would founder on a lack of recognition and so Hofmannsthal talked "as systematically as a military strategist about the necessity of conquering the major papers and forcing the old men, the opponents of this young literature, out of the foremost positions in the leading publications",[7] as Salten remembered.

A recital by a society for modern literature, "Wiener Freie Bühne", in autumn 1891 offered a podium both to a programmatic speech by Friedrich Michael Fels, the chairman, and to Arthur Schnitzler. The dismayed Schnitzler, however, summarized it as: "Much applause, meaningless evening"[8]—which would also be an accurate description of the recital put on by the Enthusiasts.

Late Fame is certainly not a *roman-à-clef*, but many of the Enthusiasts' parodically drawn character traits and physiognomic characteristics may well conceal hints at the historical members of Young Vienna. Winder, a "pale little blond boy", who is referred to by the others at the table, once mockingly, once affectionately, as "child", is reminiscent of the young Hofmannsthal who, while also just a school student, attended the coffee house "in short trousers",[9] as Stefan Zweig put it. But the young Hofmannsthal was seen from the first as a "significant talent", as Schnitzler noted of the newcomer—"Knowledge, lucidity and, it seems, a real artistic sense; it's unheard of at that age"[10]—whereas Winder is the only one of the group to be overlooked as a writer. And so the "dark-haired, slightly snobbish schoolboy Hofmannsthal, who liked the sound of his own voice" is, as Reinhard Urbach points out, transformed in Schnitzler's novella "into his opposite, a shy 'little blond boy'".[11] Linsmann, "a rather more mature man", exhibits some characteristics of Peter Altenberg, the "brilliant eccentric"[12] and self-proclaimed sponger.[13] "One of life's invalids"[14] is how Altenberg introduced himself in a letter to Schnitzler in July 1894, in a phrase that applies equally to the bald Linsmann: "they squashed me, just squashed me flat". And nor does Linsmann make any bones about being a scrounger, one who borrows money "even from little Winder".

In the character of Christian, who, "with his long hair, errant tie and somewhat unsteady eyes, most distinctly embodied the old stock figure of an 'artist'", Schnitzler seems to have portrayed his own younger self. The insignias of the archetypal artist also appear in his unfinished autobiography: "Until my first years at university I carried myself with a certain not entirely unwanted carelessness. Rembrandt hat, flapping tie, long hair. Quiet disdain for anything that was considered elegant."[15]

In the no-longer-quite-so-young actress Fräulein Gasteiner, who is the only woman in the coffee house circle and who likes to play the coquette around the venerable poet, one is tempted to see, as in other works of Schnitzler's from this period, the actress Adele Sandrock, a lover of Schnitzler's between the end of 1893 and the start of 1895, i.e. at the time when he was working on *Late Fame*. Like Gasteiner, Sandrock in 1894 played the role of Jane Eyre in *The Orphan of Lowood*, a stage adaptation of Charlotte Brontë's novel completed in 1853 by the German actress and writer Charlotte Birch-Pfeiffer.

And Sandrock, too, was pleased to see herself in the role of seductress, very much to the displeasure of Schnitzler, who in his diary soon recorded discomfiture at her "adventures [...] her deceptions".[16] "If you've been untrue to someone—console yourself, so have I,"[17] she let Schnitzler know in December 1893; on 2nd April 1894, he notes:

"Coquetry Dilly with Salten"—it famously didn't stop at coquetry.[18] The diva-ish charms of Sandrock, who was under contract at the Deutsches Volkstheater in Vienna in the early 1890s and became the source of repeated scandals, are brought to mind by the temperamental, capricious and, above all, overblown thespian manner of Gasteiner, who is considered too "eccentric" to fit into "regular theatre life".

Ultimately, the whole literary circle is exposed as a society of charlatans, as the venerable poet is told that practically none of them have read the *Wanderings* that they hail as a masterpiece. And in this way, as so often with Schnitzler, lies and truth, seriousness and play, and, at the end of novella—with Saxberger's return "from a short, troublesome journey to a home that he had never loved but in which he now rediscovered the soft and muffled comforts of before"—comedy and tragedy, too, flow into and are merged with one another.

The novella lay in Arthur Schnitzler's archive in the form of a typescript with handwritten corrections[19] and would presumably never have reached its readership had his literary estate not been rescued from the Nazis after the "Anschluss" of Austria to the Third Reich in 1938. "All the material was in my house in Vienna," the author's son Heinrich reported after the war in the periodical *Aufbau*, founded by exiles in New York. "As my father was one of the authors singled out in 1933 to have his work publicly burnt, there was an immediate danger that his books would be confiscated and destroyed. But the British consulate in Vienna made a dramatic intervention. A decisive role in this was played by the English student Eric Blackall." Blackall was in Vienna finishing his doctorate on Adalbert Stifter under Josef Nadler and was in touch with Olga Schnitzler, who had been divorced from the author in 1921. "Through his mediation," Heinrich Schnitzler continues, "the seal of the British government was placed on the door of the archive room, which put my father's estate under the protection of the British consul."[20]

A few weeks later, eight boxes containing manuscripts of completed and incomplete pieces, preliminary work, sketches, notes and extensive correspondence, along with four locked cupboards containing several thousand newspaper clippings and reviews of Schnitzler's publications and plays, were taken to England by the hauliers

Austro-Transport Fliedl, Heimerl & Co., and handed over to the Cambridge University Library—with which this part of the story seems to reach a happy conclusion.[21]

From the perspective of Heinrich, however, things looked rather different. His father's heir and executor, Heinrich was an actor and director and had "left Vienna three weeks before the so-called Anschluss to meet a film commitment in Brussels",[22] and so could not exert a direct influence on what his mother was doing with the estate. The correspondence between the two[23] initially mentions the preparations to save the material only obliquely, "in that secret language that the Nazis have forced on us", as Olga Schnitzler later said, so as not under any circumstances to jeopardize their plans.[24]

But after the papers had arrived in Cambridge—Olga, too, had meanwhile left Austria—the open but often also contentious exchange between mother and son unmistakably shows that Heinrich wanted at almost any cost to have the estate sent on to New York and deposited at Columbia University.[25]

But in line with Heinrich's fears for unpublished parts of the estate, the typescript "Story of a venerable poet", which forms the basis of this book under the title first envisaged by Arthur Schnitzler himself (*Late Fame*), remained "buried" in the archive.[26] Arthur had died on 21st October 1931. In his will, he instructed that after his death his substantial journals be transcribed by his long-standing "typewriter", Frieda Pollak, who had been continuously employed by him since 1909, all with a view to eventual publication. The will also left Heinrich free to publish parts of the estate at any time.[27] Indeed, archive texts, particularly short stories, started to appear not long afterwards in newspapers and periodicals.[28] But it was soon feared that too much would be released: "some things have to be held back—so as to always have the possibility of income from newspapers— otherwise things will look bleak one day," Olga warned her son on 16th December 1931.[29]

Among the unpublished works was the novella presented here. The typescript of the finished piece is in a capital italic face throughout, produced almost entirely without typographical errors, and contains a few cursive handwritten corrections (that have been taken in in this edition).[30]

Various typescripts in capital italics, most of them with a short note from Heinrich on the envelope, are preserved in the archive. "Typescript February 1932/unpublished", he wrote, for example, on the cover of the story "Das Himmelsbett",[31] from 1893, while on that of, say, the story "Belastet",[32] written in 1885/86, he marked: "Read on 3rd April 1933/not for publication". And the novella presented here also remained unpublished, albeit without a corresponding remark on the cover.

The story of the text's origins goes back to the last decade of the nineteenth century. A note surviving in a typescript of a list of "characters" records: "An old poet currying favour with the young generation".[33] Schnitzler then wrote in one of his papers: "Old writer who finally finds a circle of young people who 'appreciate' him. A touching figure (perhaps also incidental characters)."[34] "The impulse to start work always came from his being struck by something", is how Reinhard Urbach explains Schnitzler's typical modus operandi: "a character, a feeling, an idea, a situation, an act; a detail, a phrase, a point"—elements thrown down cursorily onto the page and then developed into a treatment, a sketch, usually several pages long and already being imagined in detail. This, too, survives: a four-page typescript[35] fully mapping out the content of the novella with some minor variations in plot development, especially towards the end. Schnitzler's "gift was not for the single stroke, but for the laborious path from the first note-making to the final draft. His talent was for revision", writes Urbach.[36]

The genesis and precise draft phases of *Late Fame* can no longer be reconstructed, as the typescript is the only surviving version in Schnitzler's estate. The process of its creation, however, can be at least rudimentarily pieced together from entries in Schnitzler's diary: "Started *Late Fame*,"[37] he writes on 30th March 1894, and, three weeks later, on 19th April: "Am hard at work on my novella".[38] Then, after only a few months, on 7th September, he seems to have completed a draft: "Read through *Late Fame*; seems to have turned out not at all badly."[39] Schnitzler next mentions the text on 8th December 1894 and records that he is considering a different title: "This afternoon read my novella 'Story of an Old Poet' to myself."[40] That this is the same text is clearly indicated by the four-page treatment mentioned above, which still carries the title "Late Fame". On Boxing Day of the same year, the diary entry reads: "Loris, Schwarzkopf, Rich[ard Beer-Hofmann], Salten at mine. Read out 'Story of an Old Poet'. More than 3 hours—went down very well; some longueurs, some styl[istic] sloppinesses, end not sad enough."[41] But Schnitzler kept working on it. Half a year later, on 22nd May 1895, he writes that he has "finished correcting" his novella "Story of an Old Poet".[42]

On 5th July 1895 in Prague, Schnitzler read the end of the story to his friend and lover Marie Reinhardt, who played a greater role than anyone else in his work and in whose judgement he had almost limitless faith. It is the ending that in the final version differs most from the initial sketch. Indeed, there were evidently further, last-minute changes, as is revealed by a letter written to Reinhardt from Bad Ischl on 17th July 1895: "This morning, darling, I finally finished my tale of the venerable poet, have cut some more and already sent it to Bahr."[43]

Schnitzler considered the novella ready to go into print and wanted Hermann Bahr to publish it serially in the periodical *Die Zeit*, of which he was one of the founders and editors. Bahr had already asked Schnitzler for a contribution in a letter of 19th June 1895: "I would very, very much like to have something from you for *Die Zeit*. Ideally a short story, not more than eight columns of the paper." If necessary, however, he would also take something longer, albeit with the proviso that "being pulled apart into instalments kills even the strongest pieces". On 17th July 1895, Schnitzler sent the desired contribution from Ischl: "so here is the novella. I've cut a lot, but still fear that it's too long. [...] If you find sections that you consider dispensable, perhaps point them out to me, but do not cut any yourself. And if a more powerful title occurs to me, I'll be very grateful."[44] Once Bahr had read the novella, first upon its arrival and then again after a few days, he responded with criticisms and asserted "as an editor" that "dismemberment into, say, eight parts, with breaks of a week" would "damage the novella and rob it of all its force".[45] Bahr suggests "shortening it by a third"—something that was never done. And so the novella sank, as Heinrich had feared for other parts of the estate, into "the long slumber of a Sleeping Beauty".[46]

WILHELM HEMECKER

AND DAVID ÖSTERLE

NOTES

1   University Library, Cambridge (ULC), Schnitzler Papers, Folder A 212,6. Cf. Gerhard Neumann, Jutta Müller, *Der Nachlass Arthur Schnitzlers* (Munich, 1969), p. 67.

2   Arthur Schnitzler's diary, 17th April 1880, p. 42. Published with the collaboration of Peter Michael Braunwarth by the Kommission für literarische Gebrauchsformen der Österreichischen Akademie der Wissenschaften. The following references are to the volumes 1879–92 (Vienna, 1897) and 1893–1902 (Vienna, 1989).

3   Schnitzler's diary, 2nd January 1880, p. 18.

4   See on this Wilhelm Hemecker and David Österle, "Café S. Griensteidl. Loris und das Junge Wien", in *Hofmannsthal Orte. 20 biographische Erkundungen*, published by Wilhelm Hemecker and Konrad Heumann (Vienna, 2014), pp. 92–116.

5   Schnitzler's diary, 26th February 1891, p. 318.

6   Schnitzler's diary, 3rd December 1892, p. 394.

7   Felix Salten, "Aus den Anfängen. Erinnerungsskizzen", in *Jahrbuch deutscher Bibliophilen-Gesellschaft* 18/19 (1932/33), pp. 31–46, p. 36.

8   Schnitzler's diary, 28th October 1891, p. 354.

9   Stefan Zweig, *Die Welt von Gestern. Erinnerungen eines Europäers* (Frankfurt, 1970), p. 64.

10 Schnitzler's diary, 29th March 1891, p. 321.

11 Reinhard Urbach, "Einen Jux wollt er sich machen", in *Die Presse*, 23rd May 2014.

12 Arthur Schnitzler, *Jugend in Wien*, edited by Therese Nickl and Heinrich Schnitzler (Vienna, 1981), p. 213.

13 Cf. Peter Altenberg, *Semmering 1912* (Berlin, 1913), p. 36.

14 Cited in Andrew Barker and Leo A. Lensing, *Peter Altenberg. Rezept, die Welt zu sehen* (Vienna, 1995), p. 48.

15 Schnitzler, *Jugend in Wien*, p. 326.

16 Schnitzler's diary, 11th April 1894, p. 74.

17 Schnitzler's diary, 6th December 1893, p. 60.

18 Schnitzler's diary, 2nd April 1894, p. 74.

19 ULC Schnitzler Papers, Folder A 164,2.

20 Heinrich Schnitzler, "Der Nachlass meines Vaters", in *Aufbau*, 9th November 1951, p. 9f.

21 See Lorenzo Bellettini and Christian Stauffenbiel, "The Schnitzler Nachlass Saved by a Cambridge Student", in *Schnitzler's Hidden*

Manuscripts, edited by L.B. and Peter Hutchinson (Oxford, 2010), pp. 11–21.

22 Heinrich Schnitzler, "'Ich bin kein Dichter, ich bin Naturforscher.' Der Nachlass meines Vaters", in *Die Neue Zeitung* (Munich), Nr. 247 (20th/21st October 1951), pp. 9–10 (p. 9).

23 The correspondence has not been published and can be found in the Heinrich Schnitzler Estate in the Österreichisches Theatermuseum (ÖTM) and in the partial Arthur Schnitzler Estate in the Deutsches Literaturarchiv in Marbach am Neckar (DLA).

24 Letter from Olga to Heinrich of 5th February 1939, DLA, A: Schnitzler, 85.1.5432/3.

25 For a comprehensive account of this, see Wilhelm Hemecker and David Österle, "'… so grundfalsch war alles Weitere'. Zur Geschichte des Nachlasses von Arthur Schnitzler", in *Jahrbuch der deutschen Schillergesellschaft* 58 (2014), pp. 3–40.

26 Cf. letter from Heinrich to Olga of 18th November 1938, ÖTM, Schn 49/6/29/1. The typescript is listed as archived in the ULC and the DLA. See also: Gerhard Neumann, Jutta Müller: *Der Nachlass Arthur Schnitzlers*, p. 105; *Arthur Schnitzler: Entworfenes und Verworfenes. Aus dem Nachlass*, edited by Reinhard Urbach, Frankfurt 1977, p. 513.

27 Arthur Schnitzler's testamentary instructions, in Neumann and Müller, *Der Nachlass Arthur Schnitzlers*, pp. 21–38, p. 36.

28 See Richard H. Allen, *An Annotated Arthur Schnitzler Bibliography. Editions and Criticism in German, French and English 1879–1965* (Chapel Hill, NC, 1966), p. 42f.

29 Letter from Olga to Heinrich of 16th December 1931, ÖTM.

30   In line with the publisher's wishes, orthography and punctuation largely follow the rules in force at the time.

31   ULC Schnitzler Papers, A 166,6.

32   ULC Schnitzler Papers, A 156.

33   ULC Schnitzler Papers, A 233,1.

34   ULC Schnitzler Papers, A 164,1.

35   Printed with standard orthography in Schnitzler, *Entworfenes und Verworfenes* (Frankfurt, 1977), p. 173f.

36   Reinhard Urbach, Preface to *Arthur Schnitzler: Entworfenes und Verworfenes*, III.

37   Schnitzler's diary, 30th March 1894, p. 73.

38   Schnitzler's diary, 19th April 1894, p. 74.

39   Schnitzler's diary, 7th September 1894, p. 86.

40   Schnitzler's diary, 8th December 1894, p. 103.

41   Schnitzler's diary, 26th December 1894, p. 107.

42   Schnitzler's diary, 22nd May 1895, p. 141. The envelope for the typescript does, however, record the period in which the work was written: '31/III–31/V 1894'.

43   *Arthur Schnitzler: Letters 1875–1912*, edited by Therese Nickl and Heinrich Schnitzler (Frankfurt, 1984), p. 267.

44   *The Letters of Arthur Schnitzler to Hermann Bahr*, edited, annotated and with an introduction by Donald G. Daviau (Chapel Hill, NC, 1978), p. 58.

45   ULC Schnitzler Papers, B 5b.

46   Letter from Heinrich to Olga of 9th March 1939, ÖTM, Schn 49/7/23; DLA, A: Schnitzler, 85.1.5380/13.

PUSHKIN PRESS

Pushkin Press was founded in 1997, and publishes novels, essays, memoirs, children's books—everything from timeless classics to the urgent and contemporary.

This book is part of the Pushkin Collection of paperbacks, designed to be as satisfying as possible to hold and to enjoy. It is typeset in Monotype Baskerville, based on the transitional English serif typeface designed in the mid-eighteenth century by John Baskerville. It was litho-printed on Munken Premium White Paper and notch-bound by the independently owned printer TJ International in Padstow, Cornwall. The cover, with French flaps, was printed on Colorplan Pristine White paper. The paper and cover board are both acid-free and Forest Stewardship Council (FSC) certified.

Pushkin Press publishes the best writing from around the world—great stories, beautifully produced, to be read and read again.

STEFAN ZWEIG · EDGAR ALLAN POE · ISAAC BABEL

TOMÁS GONZÁLEZ · ULRICH PLENZDORF · TEFFI

VELIBOR ČOLIĆ · LOUISE DE VILMORIN · MARCEL AYMÉ

ALEXANDER PUSHKIN · MAXIM BILLER · JULIEN GRACQ

BROTHERS GRIMM · HUGO VON HOFMANNSTHAL

GEORGE SAND · PHILIPPE BEAUSSANT · IVÁN REPILA

E.T.A. HOFFMANN · ALEXANDER LERNET-HOLENIA

YASUSHI INOUE · HENRY JAMES · FRIEDRICH TORBERG

ARTHUR SCHNITZLER · ANTOINE DE SAINT-EXUPÉRY

MACHI TAWARA · GAITO GAZDANOV · HERMANN HESSE

LOUIS COUPERUS · JAN JACOB SLAUERHOFF

PAUL MORAND · MARK TWAIN · PAUL FOURNEL

ANTAL SZERB · JONA OBERSKI · MEDARDO FRAILE

HÉCTOR ABAD · PETER HANDKE · ERNST WEISS

PENELOPE DELTA · RAYMOND RADIGUET · PETR KRÁL

ITALO SVEVO · RÉGIS DEBRAY · BRUNO SCHULZ